DOUBLE FUDGE & DANGER

---

a Cambria Clyne mystery

Erin Huss

To my beautiful daughter Natalie, who endured many years of apartment tours, move-out inspections, and long office hours. I love you!

Acknowledgements:

A huge thank-you to Gemma Halliday, Susie Halliday, and everyone at Gemma Halliday Publishing. To Jed, Natalie, Noah, Ryder, Emma, and Fisher, you are my motivation in all things. Thank you to my beta readers Ashley Denton, Nicole Laverne, and Blaine Tavish; Cody Christiansen for being my go-to lawyer; Ashley Stock for my author photo; everyone at Cozy Mystery Mingle for your input and support.

I underwent a prophylactic bilateral mastectomy while editing this book. The entire process—from diagnosis to surgery—was one of the hardest things I've ever had to do, and I want to thank my readers for your kind thoughts and prayers. They meant everything to me. Thank you to my author tribe, my friends, family, and especially Dr. Leslie Memsic and Dr. Georgeanna Huang for taking great care of me. There's no way I would have had the mental and physical health required to keep writing if I weren't in such great hands.

PROLOGUE

We all have fears. You know it. I know it. If monsters are hiding under the bed like my daughter thinks they are, then they know it too. There are the small conquerable fears. For me it's elevators. A tiny box suspended above the ground by thin cables—no thanks. If stairs are available, I *will* take them. Unless I'm going to the tenth floor. Then I'm able to look fear right in the face and say "Not today, fear" and hyperventilate the entire ride up.

There are the deep-seated emotional fears. For example, Tom, my baby daddy, who has a fear of commitment. Or maybe it's rejection. Or maybe it's failure. Or maybe it's all the above. Whatever the fear, it drives me bonkers.

Then there are the unspeakable fears. A threat to our survival, or worse, a threat to those we love most. The type of fear that ignites the fight or flight within and drives you to make desperate and even deadly decisions.

This is what makes my job *interesting*.

As an apartment manager, I'm privy to all my residents' freak flags, secrets, and fears. Whether I want to be or not.

Trust me. It's not a job for the delicate, bad-tempered, or anyone prone to panic attacks. It's a job for me…or at least I thought it was until I woke up in the back of an ambulance with a gunshot wound.

Now, I'm not so sure.

It might be time to quit.

CHAPTER ONE

———

—Lessons I've learned since I became an apartment manager: the term emergency *is subjective.*

"It's back on!" I ran to the couch with my bowl of ice cream, careful not to knock down the fans strategically placed around my living room. "Everyone, quiet." I unmuted the television, sat beside my daughter, Lilly, and handed her a napkin to wrap around her ice cream cone.

Celebrity Tango, a dance competition pairing sort-of celebrities with hot professional dancers, was on. My best friend, Amy Montgomery, was a sort-of celebrity and had managed to clumsily dance her way into America's hearts. No one, Amy included, anticipated her making it past week one. She lacked rhythm, grace, and popularity. Vegas gave her +2500 odds to win at the beginning of the season. I had no idea what that meant exactly, since I'd never gambled (you kind of need money to bet money), but I'd been told it wasn't good. And now Vegas could shove it, because Amy was on fire!

All that stood between her and the semifinals were a former NFL quarterback, a former soap star, a former boy band member, and an Argentine tango. This had to be celebrated.

And celebrate we did.

If celebrating meant eating ice cream, watching the show on my non-high-def TV with my maintenance man, his wife, my neighbor, and my three-year-old daughter while six fans were going at high speed around us, because it was June and 110 degrees inside my apartment—then, yeah, we were celebrating.

My name is Cambria Clyne, and I'm an on-site apartment manager slash party animal.

I ate a spoonful of double fudge ice cream, crisscrossed my legs, and stared at the television, feeling excited and proud. I already knew the results. The show had taped earlier, and Amy had sent me a text saying Raven (the former soap star and this season's favorite to win) had been sent home in a shocking elimination.

No one else at the party knew.

The *Celebrity Tango* logo flashed across the screen. Dom Astroid, a fifty-something former child star with skinny eyebrows and a helmet of dark hair, was this season's host. He flashed a movie star smile and told a few corny jokes that elicited a giggle from Lilly. Then he introduced Amy and her partner. The two took center stage. Amy looked nervous but happy. Her partner looked extra bronzed and determined. The music started, and they began to tango.

"I can't believe how much she's improved," I said in awe. "There's no way she'd be able to do that turn week one."

"Sure she's improved," said Kevin. "But this choreography is crap. They'll get a seven at most." Kevin was my neighbor. His parents owned the building—making them my boss's boss's boss. But Kevin had been disowned years ago and held no weight in decision-making around there. Otherwise, the new air-conditioning units I'd lobbied for might have been approved, and I wouldn't be sitting in a pool of sweat.

"The choreography isn't crap. It's art." I pointed the remote at the television. "They're supposed to be in an interrogation room. *He* is the detective, and Amy is the person of interest. He's coaxing the truth out of her with a sexy man shimmy. They get a—" I caught myself before I spoiled the ending. "I imagine they'll get a decent score."

An eight. They get an eight!

"There's nothing sexy about a man shimmy," Mrs. Nguyen (pronounced *when*) piped in.

She and her husband, Mr. Nguyen, lived on-site and were Lilly's stand-in grandparents since her real grandparents weren't local. Mr. Nguyen was also our trusty maintenance man. I couldn't pronounce their first names, so we kept it formal. "And what happened to his shirt? Can't the show afford buttons? Why do I need to see his belly button?"

"That's how kids wear clothes today," Mr. Nguyen added. "Nothing to the imagination."

Lilly looked up at me with her big hazel eyes. "What does *man shimmy* mean?"

"It's this." Kevin puffed his chest and gave it a shake.

Lilly made a face. "Oh yeah, that's not sexy."

I tucked a dark curl behind her ear. "Don't say *sexy*."

Lilly pushed my hand away. "Why not?"

"It doesn't sound right coming out of a three-year-old's mouth."

"Can me say *shimmy*?"

"It's *I*, and sure."

"Yay." Lilly did a shimmy then licked the dribble of ice cream slithering down her cone.

"Speaking of sexy. Amy's partner is *hot*." Kevin whistled. "What's his status?"

"He's way too young for you." Mrs. Nguyen positioned herself in front of a fan and pulled at her shirt. "And he doesn't even have chest hair yet."

"I think they wax," I said. "Also, Kevin, he's married."

"To a man or woman?"

"Does it matter?"

Kevin thought this over. "Guess not. He's in New York, and I'm in LA. The distance thing wouldn't work."

I rolled my eyes. Kevin was a good-looking guy. Auburn hair peppered with a few strands of gray. His face had strong, well-defined masculine features, and his physique was less scrawny now that he was sober. But he had terrible taste in men. I had pasty skin, a face full of freckles, blue eyes, and dark hair that I'd nicknamed Einstein. Not because of its intelligence, but because it resembled Albert Einstein's do. And I had great taste in men.

Mostly.

Amy and her partner continued their seductive interrogation and twirled around the dance floor. She looked terrific—slender, her blonde and teal hair slicked into a tight bun, and her ordinarily skeletal frame had definition for the first time in the twenty years I'd known her.

Dancing does a body good.

I looked down at my stomach and poked my gut, watching the tip of my finger disappear. Ice cream doesn't do a body good.

I had a bad habit of eating my feelings.

If you had my job, you'd eat your feelings too.

My cell buzzed in my back pocket, and I paused the television. Everyone did a collective "hey!" while I glanced at my phone. It was the emergency line. *Crap.* I thunked the heel of my hand against my forehead.

During my stint as an apartment manager, I'd learned the term *emergency* was subjective. Last week I'd received a three AM call from a resident because the wind was too loud.

FYI: not an emergency.

I placed the phone to my ear and waited for the automated recording. "You have a call on the after-hours emergency line. To accept, please press one." The robotic operator had a pleasant British accent.

I did as instructed and waited until I was connected before saying, "This is Cambria."

"We have a flood in our apartment!" a woman cried.

FYI: this *is* an emergency.

I handed Kevin my bowl of ice cream and shot upright. "Can you see where the water is coming from?"

"It's raining down from the ceiling in the master bathroom!"

In the background I could hear droplets splattering against the linoleum.

Great.

Water from the ceiling meant I had two flooded apartments. I sandwiched the phone between my ear and shoulder while I slipped on my shoes. "I'm on my way. Which apartment are you in?"

"Apartment 105."

Hal-le-lujah!

I kicked off my shoes. I managed a 40-unit apartment building in Los Angeles, and starting tomorrow, I also managed a 32-unit apartment building in Burbank. In short, no Apartment 105 under my stewardship and I could continue to party.

"Sorry, you have the wrong number," I said.

"No. I meant to call *you*!"

"We don't have an Apartment 105." I grabbed my bowl of ice cream from Kevin. "You called the wrong emergency line."

"No, I didn't. I live next door, and I called the manager's cell, and she's not answering. I need help!"

"Did you go to Violet's apartment?" Violet Pumpkin was the property manager next door. We'd conversed on several occasions. Mostly during market surveys. I'd call and ask her what her current prices were and how many vacancies she had. All the other managers on my survey list either tiptoed around the last question, or they'd tell me they were at full occupancy. Then I'd ask the mailman, and he'd give me the real number. But not Violet. She'd give me her actual vacancy percentage, talk about decreased foot traffic, what advertising methods were working for her, and which weren't. She was open and honest. A real team player.

"We did, and she didn't answer," the caller said.

"How long ago did you call her?"

"It's been at least five minutes."

Good grief. "You need to give her time to get back to you."

"I don't have *time*. There's water coming from the ceiling."

Good point.

I covered the receiver and looked at Kevin. "There's a leak in an apartment next door. They can't get a hold of Violet."

"Not your circus. Not your monkeys," he said.

True. I had my own circus and plenty of monkeys to deal with.

"Have they tried Antonio?" asked Mr. Nguyen. "He lives on-site."

Right, the maintenance man. "Did you try Antonio?"

There was a pause. "No, I haven't. But—"

"If I were you, I'd go knock on his door and tell him what's going on."

"OK, but—"

"I'm positive Violet will call you shortly. She's always on top of things. If she doesn't get back to you soon, you can call a plumber."

"Call a *plumber*," the woman echoed in disgust, as if I'd suggested she don a red wig, move to New York, and try out for a Broadway production of *Annie*. "Do you know how much I pay in rent? I shouldn't have to call a plumber myself! I shouldn't have to call around to get help! I shouldn't have a leaking ceiling!"

"I understand your frustration, and I wish you luck. Good night." I hung up before she could continue to yell. I was trying this new thing where I didn't allow other people to take out their frustration on me.

Especially when it's not even my monkey.

I searched through the contacts on my phone and found Violet's cell number. My call went straight to voicemail, which meant Violet was probably on the other line already dealing with the leak.

Good.

I pointed the remote at the television and pushed Play.

Amy finished her tango with a dip and a megawatt smile. The crowd cheered. Amy beamed. Her partner did a fist pump. The two hugged. The camera zoomed in on Amy's boyfriend, Spencer, who was in the audience, on his feet clapping. The judges prepared their scores, when my phone rang. The emergency line, again. I gave my forehead another *thunk*. Pressed Pause. Everyone went, "Hey!"

"You have a call on the after-hours emergency line. To accept, please press one."

I did as instructed and waited to be connected. "This is Cambria."

"Cambria!" It was Julia in Apartment 15. I recognized her voice. "Someone is trying to break into my apartment."

I sat up. "Someone is breaking into your apartment right now, or someone *broke* into your apartment, past tense?" Surely she had to mean the latter, because if it were the former, why would she call me? Yes, I watched a lot of cop shows. But, as I'd been reminded many times, that didn't make me an actual cop.

"Someone *is* breaking in. He's on my patio knocking on the door and trying to get in. But...oh, wait...he's gone."

"Where'd he go? Or even better, how'd he get on your patio?" Julia lived upstairs.

"I have no idea how he got up here but...wait...he's on the roof."

"Are you sure?"

"Yeah, I'm looking out my front window and can see someone running across the roof."

Good grief.

"Julia, listen to me carefully. Stay in your apartment. I'll be right there." I put on my shoes and grabbed my keys.

"Where are you going?" Mr. Nguyen asked.

"This one is my circus, and I've got a monkey on the roof! No maintenance required! Can you stay here with Lilly?"

"No need to yell anymore." He pointed to the hearing aid wrapped around his ear. A new development.

Sorry, I mouthed. "I forgot." The Nguyens had been hard of hearing since I'd met them. Old habits die hard.

"No apology. Go. Go." Mrs. Nguyen plopped down on the couch beside Lilly and positioned a fan in front of them.

"I'm coming with you," Kevin said. He didn't bother putting his shoes on, being that he wasn't wearing any when he arrived. He wasn't wearing a shirt either.

Clothing wasn't really his thing.

I ran through the first courtyard with my phone ringing in my ear and Kevin trailing behind. "9-1-1 dispatch. What is your emergency?"

"I'm an apartment manager, and one of my residents reported a man attempted to break into her apartment, and he's now on the roof." I stopped in the breezeway and peeked around the corner. Kevin ran up behind me, struggling to catch his breath.

Exercise wasn't really his thing either.

The building was split up into three courtyards with ivy-laced breezeways connecting them. It was your typical seventies-inspired construction. Brown fascia. Tan stucco. Black iron railings. Brownish-greenish grass. Nothing spectacular, but clean, and I loved living there.

Mostly.

Apartment 15 overlooked the pool in the second courtyard. Below, and tucked around a corner, was Apartment 13. (The building wasn't numbered in order. Why? No idea. Drugs were popular the 70s. Maybe the architect was high.) Daniella lived in Apartment 13 with her pet tarantula. She was a feisty little thing with dark hair and lipstick on her teeth (Daniella, not the tarantula) who berated me in both English and Spanish and lived in a world where everything was my fault. If she knew a man had attempted to break into Julia's apartment, she'd leave a nasty review on Rent or Run dot com, and I'd only just got our run rate down.

Lucky for me, Daniella's door was closed and the front porch light was off. Which meant she wasn't home.

I looked up at the roof but didn't see or hear anything.

"Do you have a physical description of the man?" asked the dispatch operator.

"No." I moved the phone to my other ear and pushed open the pool gate with Kevin still behind me. It was dark, muggy, and a bit eerie. My body erupted in tiny goose bumps. Mostly because Kevin was breathing down my neck, but also because it felt as if someone was watching us and I thought I heard my name.

I pressed the phone into my chest. "Did you hear that?" I whispered to Kevin.

"Wh—"

I covered his mouth. "Someone is saying my name."

Kevin licked the inside of my hand.

"Gross."

"No one is saying your name, crazy woman. There's no one on the roof either."

I waited to be sure. Heard nothing. Wiped Kevin's spit off of my palm using the backside of my jeans. Brought the phone back to my ear and said, "I don't see anyone." I walked past the pool, pushed open the gate on the other side, and stepped into the second breezeway. "Unless they're—*ouch!*" A shoe landed on my head. Not just any shoe either. A heavy, well-worn black work boot.

I picked the boot up using my forefinger and thumb. It smelled like rum and prunes.

Kevin tapped my shoulder and pointed up. A stout man in a black T-shirt walked along the breezeway beam, with his hands out to his side, carefully shuffling along like he was walking a tightrope.

Crap.

I gave my phone to Kevin, cupped my hands around my mouth, and waited until the man had cleared the beam before I yelled, "Hey! What are you doing up there?"

The man slipped and face-planted into the shingled roof with a *thud.*

That had to hurt.

"He's still on the roof," Kevin told the operator, then looked at me. "She advised you to keep your distance and wait for the police to arrive."

"Hold on a second." I squinted up at the man. I had a hard time seeing anything other than his silhouette. Until he rose to his feet and a sliver of moonlight shone across his face. "Larry?"

The man looked down.

Yep. Larry.

Larry lived in Apartment 32. He had long, stringy gray hair, a potbelly, and suffered from chronic constipation. I knew this because he obsessively talked about it. No matter how many times I'd asked him not to.

Larry peered down at me. "Why do you have my shoe?"

"It fell on my head! What are you doing on the roof?"

"I locked myself out," he said as if it were obvious.

"And you're on the roof because?"

"'*Cause* I was on my patio when I got locked out." It was dark and hard to see, but I was fairly sure Larry rolled his eyes at me.

"The perp is five seven, two hundred and fifty-three pounds, long gray hair..." Kevin said to the operator. "He might be armed!"

I smacked Kevin on the chest with the backside of my hand. "He's not armed. Don't say that."

"You never know."

"Give that back to me." I lunged for my phone, and Kevin turned around, positioning his bare back between my cell and me. Kevin and Larry didn't get along. They'd had a falling out over a box of Girl Scout Cookies last year, and their relationship never recovered.

"Come quick," Kevin said before he hung up.

"What is wrong with you?" I yanked my phone from his grasp. "We don't need the police." Larry was many things, but he was not a criminal. Him climbing on the roof and going around to his neighbors' patios to look for help—while not the brightest idea—sounded very Larry-like. His path from *problem* to *solution* was a long squiggly line with several loop-the-loops in between.

"No talking about me behind my back!" yelled Larry.

"Dude, we're not talking behind your back, because you're facing us." Kevin gave me a this-guy's-nuts look.

"Larry, go to your patio, and I'll let you in," I said.

"No, I'll just jump." Larry crouched down like a skier about to go down the side of a mountain.

Kevin cupped his hands around his mouth. "Go for it!"

I smacked him on the chest. "Don't say that."

"Why? He's like thirty feet from the ground. Worst case he'll break a leg. No big deal."

"No one is breaking anything tonight." I looked up at Larry. "Whatever you do, don't jump. Go to your patio, and I'll let you in."

"Okey-dokey."

Larry turned around and lost his footing. I let out a yelp as I watched Larry slide down the side of the roof. I stuttered around, trying to position myself to catch him. Momentarily forgetting that I lacked the upper body strength required to catch anyone. Let alone a fifty-something-year-old man. But you heard about people developing superhuman abilities in high-adrenaline situations all the time.

Larry grabbed hold of the beam and dangled above us. I heard sirens fast approaching. "Hold on, Larry. Help is on the way."

"I…can't…hold on." His fingers slipped from the beam, and he fell in what felt like slow motion. I held out my arms, ready to catch him, and watched as he landed directly beside me.

CHAPTER TWO

———

—A drop from thirty feet can do more than break a leg.

The police arrived with guns drawn. After they made sure no one was armed (that was a fun pat down), an ambulance was called. Poor Larry looked like a pretzel, but I could see his chest move up and down and heard the profanity fly from his mouth, so I had a hunch he'd live.

The paramedic placed an oxygen mask over Larry's mouth (to get him to shut up), strapped him to a gurney, and wheeled him away. I overheard the paramedic say it appeared Larry had two broken femurs and they were taking him to County Hospital. With the siren on, the ambulance bounced down the bumpy terrain of the driveway and out of sight.

A group of residents gathered to see what all the commotion was. Per the usual, Silvia Kravitz—the community gossip and Larry's neighbor—stood in the middle of the crowd with her parrot, Harold, perched on her shoulder. Silvia was a retired actress, only wore lingerie, and looked like the seventy-year-old love child of Gollum and Joan Rivers thanks to the ten-too-many facelifts she'd had. If she *could* move her face, I think she'd appear worried. As it was, she appeared to be in a constant state of shock, like her eyeballs were moments from popping out of her head. Silvia didn't like Larry. But she didn't like anyone. I think she disliked Larry the least and me the most.

Once all emergency personnel were gone, I went to assure Julia it was only Larry on her patio, not a crazy man trying to break in.

Kevin walked at my side, picking at the skin around his nail beds. "You mad at me?"

"I'm irritated," I said, because I was. "Why'd you say Larry was armed? That wasn't necessary."

"You can never be too careful. People can stash weapons anywhere, and I mean *anywhere*."

"Gross."

"You hear things in prison. This one guy—"

"I don't need to hear the rest of that story." I walked up the stairs taking two steps at a time.

"Larry's patio faces the courtyard. He could have yelled for help. He didn't need to climb on the roof. His story doesn't make sense."

"This is Larry we're talking about." I stopped at Apartment 15 and knocked. "He got his ponytail stuck in his garbage disposal once."

"How is that possible?"

"Your guess is as good as mine."

The porch light turned on. Julia answered wearing a purple terrycloth bathrobe pulled tight around her twig frame, her magenta hair wet and slicked back. There was a beer in her hand and black goo smeared on her face. She nodded for us to come in.

Julia and her brother Kane had moved into Apartment 15 a few weeks earlier—and you could tell. No pictures on the wall. Sparsely furnished. The place still smelled of fresh paint, and the new carpet was still shedding.

"We figured out who was on your patio," I said. "You'll be happy to know it wasn't a burglar. It was a resident who had locked himself out and was looking for help."

Julia took a seat at the kitchen table, dropping onto the chair with a sigh. "It totally, like, scared the crap out of me." She paused to take a swig of beer. "I was about to take a shower, when I heard the knocking. This moron was too busy playing his stupid game and didn't even hear."

The "moron" being her brother who was on the couch with headphones on, eyes glued to the television with thumbs working the controller in his hands. Kane had yet to acknowledge our presence. Even after we walked past the television on our way to the kitchen.

"I came running out to the living room and saw some guy trying to open the door. So I told him to get off my patio or I would kill him. Then I called you."

"Just in case something like this happens again, which it shouldn't, please call 9-1-1 first," I said.

She squished her brows together as if the thought of calling 9-1-1 hadn't dawned on her.

Seemed Julia's road from *problem* to *solution* had a few loop-the-loops as well.

Kevin took a seat beside Kane, propped his feet on the coffee table, and stretched his arm along the back of the couch. Kane jumped and pushed his headphones off. "Dude! What are you doing here?" Kane turned around. "Uh...what's happening?"

"Some guy tried to break into our apartment while you were playing your stupid game," Julia said.

"He didn't try to break in. He was locked out and needed help," I said. "Do you know Larry from Apartment 32?"

Kane scratched the back of his head. "The dude with the hemorrhoids?"

Julia made a face. "Do I even want to know how you know that?"

"I talk to him in the laundry room," Kane said defensively. "We're friends. I guess."

"Which is probably why he came to your apartment for help." I gave Kevin a so-there bob of my head just as my phone buzzed from my back pocket. It was the emergency line.

What more could possibly go wrong tonight?

Once connected I placed the phone to my ear and said, "This is Cambria," and stepped out onto the walkway.

"I've knocked on the maintenance man's door multiple times. I've run all around looking for him. His car is here, but he isn't. The assistant manager doesn't live on-site. Violet still isn't answering her door or the phone. It's like the entire staff decided to take a vacation. It's ridiculous! I pay almost four thousand dollars a month, and I was just given a rental increase yesterday. A rental increase! Now all my personal belongings are damaged!"

Yikes.

Tenants didn't typically handle rental increases well. Not that I blamed them. Who wanted to pay more money for their apartment? A flood shortly *after* a rental increase was unfortunate timing for Violet.

Very unfortunate, actually.

"Do you have renters insurance?" I asked.

"Of course not! Renters insurance is a total scam."

"It's really not, and anything damaged by the leak won't be covered under the—" I snapped my mouth shut.

Not your circus. Don't give legal advice to other people's monkeys.

I had no idea what their leasing agreements entailed.

But still.

When you pay a small fortune in rent, it's a good idea to insure your personal belongings.

"Isn't there an emergency line?" I asked, still fighting the urge to run over and help.

"No! All I have is Violet's cell phone. She's not answering, and I swear the ceiling is about to come down! My son and I are using buckets to collect the water, but there's too much!"

I pinched the bridge of my nose. "What's your name?"

"Dolores Rocklynn in Apartment 105."

"OK, Dolores. This is important. If you think the ceiling is about to come down don't stand—" I heard a crash. "Dolores? Are you still there?"

"A piece of the ceiling just landed on my head! Now more water is coming down!"

"Did you go to the apartment above you and talk to them? Maybe they left the water on?"

"Violet lives right above us!"

Well, there's a tidbit of information that would have been good to know the first time around.

I leaned into Julia's apartment. Kevin now had a controller in his hand, and he and Kane were both playing the game. I asked Kevin to man the place while I went next door. I couldn't help myself. If Violet's boss found out a leak went unattended to and drywall fell on a tenant's head, then she could lose her job. Especially if the leak came from her apartment.

I asked Dolores for the entry code and told her I'd be right there. To do what? I had no idea. I wasn't a plumber. My dad was. Maybe plumbing was in my DNA and I'd know what to do when I saw the problem.

On the way over, I called Mr. Nguyen. In the past, I'd text him. Now that he had hearing aids, I could call and he'd answer on the first ring.

I asked him how Lilly was doing and gave them the go-ahead to finish *Celebrity Tango* without me.

"When are you coming back?" he asked.

"Hopefully soon. Do you have the number for the maintenance man next door?"

"Why do you need his number?"

"The resident over there still has a leak, and no one is getting back to her."

"Not your circus. Not your monkeys."

"Yeah, I know."

Does the circus even have monkeys?

I hung up, and Mr. Nguyen sent me the contact information for *Antonio MM*. Antonio didn't answer, and I left a voicemail asking him to meet me in Apartment 105.

Next door was an imposing ten-story building with a gated wraparound parking lot and an underground parking structure. Unlike my nameless complex, this place had a name: Cedar Creek Luxury Living. A cobblestoned walkway led up to a pair of whimsical wrought-iron doors. Brilliant red and yellow flowers were dispersed throughout the lavish landscaping. A koi pond glistened near the entrance, with gold and yellow fish swimming beneath the water. Large trees towered like a fortress around the perimeter, prohibiting residents and guests from seeing *my* apartment building.

Which was fine.

We offered affordability, and they offered a state-of-the-art gym, an Olympic-sized pool, washer and dryer hookups *in* the apartment, fully renovated kitchens, a theater room, a game room, a conference room, and a sauna.

It was nice, sure. But who *needs* a state-of-the-art gym anyway?

Answer: me.

I hurried down the sidewalk and—*oomph*. There was a step. A big step. A step painted red with a large hard-to-miss sign warning pedestrians of the impending step. A step I forgot was there until I was on my hands and knees and staring at it.

Honestly.

How I managed to make it twenty-nine years without accidentally killing myself had to be some kind of world record.

I stood, dusted myself off, made it to the whimsical doors without further incident, and entered the code Dolores had given me. I'd never been inside Cedar Creek before. Violet and I mainly spoke on the phone, or she'd come over. The place smelled of honey and corporate air conditioning. The leasing office was to my right behind a glass wall. A fancy espresso machine sat atop a long cabinet, and two mahogany desks adorned each side of the room. To my left was a lobby that resembled an art gallery. A vase of cherry blossoms graced the glass coffee table positioned between two low-back couches. The walls were beveled and painted a cream color, with large abstract art hung around the room. The apartment manager in me was in awe. The mom in me thought about having to clean fingerprints off those glass walls.

Apartment 105 was on the first floor. No elevator required. *Phew.* I rang the doorbell. A masculine woman wearing pink leggings with flamingo heads printed on them answered. Mascara lines stained her cheeks, her black hair was drenched into ringlets, and her face was plagued with confusion. "Who the hell are you?"

Well hello to you too.

"I'm Cambria. We talked on the phone."

She cocked her head to the side. "I heard the manager next door was old?"

"You must be thinking of the previous manager, Joyce. She retired last year, and I took over. Can I come in and take a look at the problem?" I felt a bit intrusive asking, until I remembered *she* was the one who called *me*—not once, but twice!

"I got it under control now," she said.

Under control?

Over her shoulder I could see the water slithering down the hallway and into the living room. And what a beautiful living room it was. Plush couches. Persian rugs. Expensive-looking trinkets. A darn shame none of it was insured.

Typically, tenants would exaggerate the damage to rush management over. Dolores had not been exaggerating.

Not exaggerating one bit.

"So you talked to Violet?" I asked, trying to understand. "She's taking care of it?"

"No! That woman is a horrible manager. The worst I've ever had."

Geez. "Then you got a hold of Antonio?"

"No. That man is a horrible maintenance supervisor. The worst I've ever had."

OK. "A plumber?"

She blinked a few times. "Yes. A plumber will be here soon. It's best to leave it to the professionals, sweetie," she said, her tone mocking. "Good night." She closed the door and flipped the lock.

Well, OK then.

Clearly she was expecting Joyce. Which, sure, Joyce was nice and all, but she was also like a hundred years old, smoked a pack a day, and couldn't walk five feet without folding over into a coughing fit. Why not give the new manager a try? I was young, and spry (kind of), and, dammit, I have plumbers' DNA!

Whatever.

It didn't matter.

What *did* matter was the concerning amount of water coming from Violet's apartment, and the fact that Dolores had not been able to get a hold of her. Violet could be hurt or…worse.

Yikes.

I ran down the hall and followed the *Exit* signs until I found the stairwell. This was an emergency. No time for the elevator. I took the steps two at a time with my phone at my ear, trying Antonio's number again. It went straight to voicemail. "This is Cambria Clyne. There's a leak in Apartment 105, and it's coming from Violet's apartment. Can you please meet me there and let me in, ASAP?"

I shoved my phone into my back pocket and held tight to the railing as I trekked up the stairs. I'm a klutz. And falling down two flights of stairs did not sound like a fun way to die. Cedar Creek charged 4,000 dollars for a one-bedroom apartment. You'd think they could afford anti-slip grip on their steps. It was like climbing a staircase made of ice. Also, I was out of breath.

Note to self: Work out, woman. This is pathetic.

The second-floor door to the stairwell swung open. A person in a sweatshirt with the hood pulled over his head bolted down the stairs, rammed me with his shoulder, and kept going. I lost my footing and landed on my knee. A sharp pain shot up my leg, rendering me momentarily paralyzed.

I poked my head through the railing. "If you live here, then you can certainly afford some manners," I hollered after the man.

He stopped and looked up at me with brown eyes but offered no apology. Then he turned, pushed open the door to the first floor, and disappeared.

Real nice!

I took a few breaths, shed a tear or two, said a few curse words, limped up the remaining steps to the second floor, and found the sign pointing to the manager's apartment.

Antonio, the maintenance man, booked it around the corner with a toolbox and shop vac in his hands and almost crashed into me. He was an older guy and wore jean shorts and a tight white tank top. Two gold chains hung around his neck and were buried deep in his curly chest hairs.

"There you are." I held him by the arm to regain my balance and gently put pressure on my knee again. "You got my message."

"What happened to you?" he asked.

"One of your residents ran me over in the stairwell."

"Why are you in the stairwell?"

"I don't like elevators. There's no time for chitchat. Let's get to Violet's apartment." I hobbled forward. With each step the pain in my knee grew more manageable until I was able to walk like a human and not a crazy-haired zombie. We stopped at the apartment labeled *Manager.*

"So what you doing here?" Antonio flipped through his giant key ring.

"Violet didn't answer her cell."

Antonio shoved his key into the top deadbolt lock. "Huh..."

"What's wrong?" I asked.

"It's unlocked." Antonio pushed opened the door and peeked in. "Hello? It's Antonio with the apartment manager from next door. Hello?"

No answer.

I shoved Antonio out of the way and stuck my face into the apartment, not wanting to enter just yet. "Violet!" I tried. Still nothing. The nightly news was on the large television mounted to the wall. The reporter had a microphone up to Raven's mouth, the newly booted contestant from *Celebrity Tango*, asking her about the shocking elimination. I didn't pay attention to her response. I was too distracted by the apartment.

Violet Pumpkin was in her early fifties, or mid-sixties (I sucked at age guesstimation). She had dark wavy hair, blue eyes, and impossibly long lashes. She'd been an apartment manager for thirty years and loved her job. Like me, she was a single mother. We had swapped stories of how difficult it was to manage with a small child at home. She gave me hope, because while I was still in the trenches of parenthood, Violet's daughter had graduated from UCLA and worked in Florida at a pharmaceutical company. She had a husband, two children, a big house with a pool, and, according to Violet, was a fully functioning and happy member of society. Which was what I wanted for Lilly.

Violet gave me a glimpse into what my future could be. If I worked hard, someday I could manage a luxury apartment building, have a happy, successful daughter, and, *wow*, a gorgeous home.

Violet's style was classic. Instead of a couch, she had high-back cream-colored chairs configured around a circular blue ottoman. A dark hutch filled with teal and silver vases, modern trinkets, and a row of succulents. Sure, the view was terrible. Through the large windows, all I saw was my complex, which was a bummer for her. But when you live in the heart of LA, it's not like you're getting an ocean view.

My apartment was mostly made up of the furnishings residents left behind when they moved. Violet clearly made a better living than I did. Which made sense. She'd been doing it longer and sold luxury. I'd been doing it less than a year and sold shedding carpet.

I pushed the door all the way open and noticed the footprint beneath the knob. I checked the doorframe and ran my fingers along the fresh scratches. A feeling of dread slithered through my stomach.

Someone had kicked in the door.

"Violet!" I dashed inside. Nothing appeared to be missing or out of place. Except her purse and phone were on the kitchen counter.

Crap.

Into the master bedroom I went, my heart slamming against my chest. The bathroom was through a short, mirrored hallway, and, *holy crap!* It was gorgeous. Marble counters with framed mirrors. A shower with enough room for two. A jetted bathtub big enough for three. Maybe four and, oh yeah, a lake.

The bathtub was on, and water lapped over the side and spilled onto the tile. I tried to turn it off, but it was stuck.

Antonio pushed me out of the way and used a wrench to pull the lever. A vein popped out the side of his neck.

"Back up. Let me try something." I placed a hand on his shoulder and used my good leg to kick the lever as hard as I could. It budged an inch.

Well, OK, that didn't work.

Antonio dug through his toolbox and pulled out a saw and began to cut a hole in the drywall.

"Why don't you shut the water off to the building instead?" I asked.

Antonio didn't answer. Instead, he ripped out a square of drywall, revealing the water shutoff valve.

Oh, got it.

Note to self: you don't have plumber DNA.

Antonio turned the lever, and the faucet shut off.
"Phew." He wiped his brow with the back side of his hand. "I got this if you want to go. Just need to get this water cleaned up."

He grabbed the shop vacuum and plugged it into an outlet next to the sink. It whistled to life, and by whistle, I mean a high-pitched, break-a-window whistle.

"I'm worried someone broke in!" I shouted over the noise.

He looked around. "Nothing appears to be missing!"

"Where do you think Violet is? Her purse is on the counter!"

"She's probably in the office!"

"I was just down there and didn't see her! I got the first call about the water leaking over an hour ago, so she's been gone at least that long, probably more..." A metal U-shaped ring on the floor caught my attention. I yanked the vacuum cord from the wall. "What's that?" I pointed.

Antonio spun in a complete circle like he was chasing an imaginary tail. "What you talking about?"

"That! On the floor. It looks like a toilet paper holder." I held on to the counter and bent down for a closer inspection. "It *is* a toilet paper holder!" I slid open the door by the vanity and came face-to-face with a...toilet. "Why is the seat glowing?"

"It's heated."

Heated?

You've got to be kidding me.

I couldn't recall there ever being a time when I sat on the john and thought, *If only my butt cheeks were hot, this would go a lot smoother.*

Granted, I'd never sat on a heated toilet seat before. My butt didn't know what it was missing.

There was a hole where the toilet paper holder had been ripped from the wall. I squatted down and used the inside of my forearm to feel the temp of the seat. It was warm. Not sure how this was relevant, but I was curious.

"We need to call the police. I'm worried something happened to Violet. The running bathtub, the kicked in door, the toilet paper holder torn from the wall, her purse in the kitchen, the...do you feel a draft?"

"You have a hard time staying on topic."

"No, I don't." OK, maybe a little. "Do you feel that breeze?"

Antonio licked his finger and held it up. "Nope. No breeze. What I think happened is, Violet ran a bath and couldn't get the water to shut off. Now she's looking for me, and if she finds me snooping through her apartment and you feeling up her toilet seat, then she's not going to be happy."

I ignored him. "There's a window open somewhere around here." I stepped behind the shower and found a walk-in closet large enough to fit a twin bed. Shoes were scattered, boxes smashed, and clothes piled in the corners. Paperwork was sprinkled around, and a suitcase lay open and empty.

"Well I'll be damned," Antonio said, looking over my shoulder.

"I'll be damned is right. Look!" I pointed to the red stains splattered on the wall beneath the open window. "That looks like blood."

"It does." The dread in his voice matched my own.

I stepped around the suitcase, careful not to touch anything, and tiptoed to the open window. Directly outside was the fire escape. Making it easy for someone to get out, or for someone to sneak in.

Gulp.

For the record: this classified as an emergency.

CHAPTER THREE

———

—Only heavy walkers rent upstairs apartments.

I stood at the curb in front of Cedar Creek with my face pointed toward the sky. The smog had thickened, blocking the moon from my view. But I knew it was there, and I suspected it was full.

"I should move to Montana," I said to the detective at my side.

He followed my gaze. "Why?"

"I bet in Montana the sky is clear and you can see the moon, and people don't show up dead all the freaking time."

"I hate to break it to you, but people die in every state."

"Yeah, well, maybe Montanans don't murder as often because they're not sucking up so much carbon dioxide on the regular."

"You don't know that anyone has been murdered."

"Blood on the wall. Bathtub overflowing. Door kicked open. Personal belongings on the counter. Someone killed Violet. They killed her while she was going to the bathroom, and they were about to put her in the bathtub to erase all DNA evidence but got spooked when they were unable to turn off the broken faucet, and deposited her elsewhere. Which will make this case ten times more difficult to solve since you have no body, no murder weapon, and not much DNA given the bathroom, where the murder happened, is flooded."

"You need to lay off the crime shows."

"Probably." I turned to face the detective. He had on a gray suit, white shirt, and no tie. He was a little older than me. Early thirties. Dark blond hair. A scruffy jawline, a tiny scar under his left nostril, and superhuman good looks. He was also pretty much my boyfriend. Detective Chase Cruller. As in the donut. The best kind of donut. The melt-in-your-mouth, fluffy, perfectly sweet...

OK, now I want a donut.

Then I thought about Violet.

Never mind.

Sure, I didn't know Violet well. But I'd spoken to her the day before during a market survey. I'd been in her apartment. I'd seen the crime scene. She was a fellow apartment manager. She was *me* in thirty years.

It felt personal.

"I'm sorry." Chase slid his arm around my shoulders and kissed the top of my head. I leaned into his touch, and my eyes cut to the CSI vans parked in front of Cedar Creek.

"Shouldn't you be in there working?"

"Not my case. I overheard the address on the radio and came to make sure you were OK." He placed his finger under my chin and forced me to look at him. He had the most magnificent green eyes. "You OK?"

"No."

"Can I walk you home?"

"No."

"Ice cream?"

"No."

"Can I offer *other* distractions?" He winked.

I hesitated because despite all that had happened, he *did* have superhuman good looks, and I *was* merely human. Life is short. One minute you're perched upon your fancy toilet seat, and the next you're...*ugh.* "Not tonight."

Chase tucked a strand of Einstein behind my ear. "Where's Lilly?"

"Inside with Mr. and Mrs. Nguyen." I checked my watch, suddenly realizing how late it was. "I have to get her to bed, or she'll be impossible tomorrow. I'm going to sit by her window with a knife and pepper spray all night."

"Don't do that. These things are typically domestic. This is a secured building, and she lived on the second floor. Whoever did this knew Violet."

He made a point. Violet and I didn't exactly run in the same circle. Chances are if the killer knew Violet, he or she didn't know me as well.

I hoped.

"Who is the lead on this case if you're not?" I asked.

"Hampton... Why are you making that face?"

Ugh. Hampton was Chase's partner. A forty-something bald man with round glasses who was as tall as he was wide. Also, "He wears his pants too high."

"That has nothing to do with his ability to do the job."

"OK. And *maybe.* But I don't see how you can efficiently work with a wedgie?"

"Give the man a break. He's..." Chase glanced over my shoulder. "He's coming. Don't stare."

Don't stare?

I turned around and...*you've got to be kidding me.*

Hampton strode down the walkway with his arms swinging, hips swaying, mouth terse, like a man on a mission, with his pants hiked up, and his glasses on his nose, and the worst toupee I'd ever seen. Like a squirrel crawled on top of his head and died.

Chase gently jabbed his elbow into my side, forcing me to tear my eyes away from the monstrosity. And here I thought I was having a bad hair day.

"Good evening, Cambria," Hampton said, giving his pants a hike. "How are you holding up?"

"As good as can be expected," I said to the ground, concentrating on the veiny cracks in the sidewalk to keep from staring. "Have you informed Violet's daughter yet?" The thought of a sheriff pounding on her door in the middle of the night to break the news her mother was missing made me sick.

"We have someone contacting her next of kin," Hampton said. "I need to ask you some questions."

"Of course," I said, still looking at the ground. "Whatever you want to know."

Hampton adjusted his belt, clicked a pen, and proceeded to ask the details of how I came to be in Violet's apartment. I told him about the phone calls, how I had first stopped at Apartment 105, was denied access, and then met Antonio at Violet's. I assured him that neither Antonio nor I touched anything with our hands once we realized we were standing in a crime scene and that we'd immediately left the apartment and called 9-1-1.

"Why didn't Dolores let you in?" he asked.

"She said a plumber was on the way."

"Huh?" Hampton frowned.

"Why'd you 'huh'?" I asked. "Do you think she had something to do with it?" It would be odd to commit a murder, flood your own apartment, and call the neighboring apartment manager to come take care of it. But then again, I'd just had a resident fall off the roof because he locked himself out. Not everyone chooses logic.

"No," Hampton said with little conviction. "We were in her apartment, but there wasn't a plumber. The damage is quite extensive though."

Huh?

"You said the door to Violet's apartment was open," Hampton said. "Was it wide open or cracked?"

"Cracked. So whoever kicked it in closed it behind them. The closet window was open, so perhaps they went in the door and out the window. But how do you go out the window with a body or a hostage? Did you see anything in the stairwell or in the elevator?"

"CSI is processing the scene now." Hampton used one foot to scratch the back of his calf. "Anything else you can remember?"

I bent down to rub my sore kneecap, when a memory trotted into my head. "I completely forgot! As I was going up the stairs to Violet's apartment, a man in a hooded sweatshirt entered in through the second-floor stairwell door, ran me over, and exited the first story door. He didn't even stop to see if I was hurt. He could have been coming from Violet's apartment. Or maybe he's just a douchebag." The latter was indeed a possibility. Being at least 10 percent douchebag is necessary for survival when you live in Los Angeles. The timing, however, was fishy. This could have been a two-man job.

Chase squared me and stuck his hands in the front pocket of his pants. "Did you get a good look at his face?"

"I've got this." Hampton took a step between Chase and me and then stared at me with such intensity I squirmed. "Did you get a good look at this man's face?"

I closed my eyes and flipped through my memory. "A decent look. I'm pretty sure I could point him out if I were given a lineup."

Chase turned to Hampton. "They should have copies of every resident's identification on file here. You could also have her meet with the forensic sketch artist,"

Hampton put a hand on Chase's shoulder and nodded.

Chase let out a relenting sigh and nodded back.

The two had their own nodding language that I'd yet to fully decipher. My best guess was Hampton told Chase this was *his* case and to shut up. Or something to that effect, because Chase closed his mouth, took a step back, and returned his hands to the front pocket of his slacks.

"Here's what we'll do," Hampton said. Between the heat and the nodding, the blob of hair on Hampton's head had slid down to the middle of his forehead.

I must have been staring, because Chase elbowed me again. "I'm sorry." I blinked to clear the image. "What were you saying?"

Hampton adjusted his toupee. "We'll have you meet with our sketch artist."

"What about Kevin?" I said. "He's been taking classes at the college to do forensic sketches. He could do it?"

"We have an artist contracted already," Chase explained. "He's very good at what he does."

Bummer. Kevin could have used the extra income. "Do I meet with the artist now?"

"Come in tomorrow at noon." Hampton handed me a business card as if I didn't know where the station was. As if I hadn't been there many times before. As if I didn't have a job or responsibilities and could just take off in the middle of the day.

Also, noon tomorrow gave me plenty of time to forget what the man looked like.

"I don't have anything else for you at the moment." Hampton gave my arm a reassuring squeeze. "We'll do our best to bring Violet home," he said, his words sincere. He strutted back toward the whimsical doors of Cedar Creek.

I waited until he was out of earshot before I said, "You cannot let him walk around with that thing on his head. I can't believe no one has said anything to him."

"We're being supportive. He's going through stuff."

"Like what?"

"His wife left him."

"Ouch."

"For his best friend."

"Double ouch."

"And she took the dog."

"Great. Now I feel bad for staring. Should I apologize?"

"I wouldn't bring up the hair, or the wife, or the best friend, or the dog."

"Fine. But if he's having problems at home, can he be trusted to find Violet?" Time is of the essence in a missing person case. I'd learned that from my crime shows. The first forty-eight hours are critical, and I didn't trust Hampton to make good decisions when he couldn't even be trusted to dress himself. "Can you take this case? As a favor to me. Please?"

Chase massaged the back of his neck. He only did this when he was about to deliver bad news. "I have to go on a business trip. I'm leaving tonight, and I'll be gone for two days."

"Where?"

"Texas."

"Texas! You live in California! You work for the LAPD! Why are you going to *Texas*?"

Chase glanced over his shoulder at his colleagues, who were now all staring at us.

Oops.

I cleared my throat, smoothed out my shirt, and spoke more quietly. "What is in Texas?"

"It's a special assignment."

Great. My stomach clenched. Chase's job was dangerous enough without any secret special assignments.

Chase cupped my cheeks in his hands. "Don't worry," he said, reading my thoughts. "It's nothing dangerous."

Pfft. Like he'd tell me if it was.

The truth was, Chase was a detective. I knew this going into the relationship. What was I going to say?

Don't go. Don't do your job. Stay here with me because I'm afraid there's a lunatic out there kidnapping apartment managers?

I'd never get between Chase and his job. Just as I hope he'd never get in the way of me doing mine.

Of course, I rented apartments, and he fought bad guys. But still.

"Go home and rest." Chase placed his hands on my hips. "You've got a big day tomorrow."

Big day? "You mean because of the sketch artist?"

"Don't you start at the Burbank building tomorrow?"

Oh, right. That. "I also have to check on Larry because he fell off the roof and broke his femurs."

Chase's eyebrows shot up. "Why was he on the roof?"

"Locked himself out."

"Is this the constipated guy?"

"The one and only."

Chase laughed. Larry was a hard guy to forget. "I don't know who has a crazier job. Me or you."

"You and I both know it's me." I rose to my toes and kissed Chase. His lips on mine turned my legs to goo, just as they did the first time I laid eyes on him. It was still hard to comprehend such a glorious specimen of a man was interested in *me*. And for a moment, all I could think about was the taste of his mouth, the feel of his tongue, the heat of his hands on my face and hard body pressed against mine.

Someone hollered for us to "get a room," and I was brought back to reality.

Making out at a crime scene is probably tacky anyhow.

"I'll see you Thursday." Chase kissed my cheek and sauntered away. It wasn't until his butt was out of my sight that I remembered *why* we were standing in a crime scene—Violet was gone.

* * *

After I put Lilly to bed, I sat at my desk and sent Patrick, my boss, an email about Larry falling from the roof. My cell rang ten minutes later. "Please tell me you're joking."

"I wish I was."

Patrick made a noise. I couldn't tell if he was laughing or sighing or crying or all the above. He'd been in the property management business for a long time. Too long, he'd told me once…or twice. "Make a detailed report for the file."

"Already on it." I shook the mouse to wake the computer and clicked *Print* on the document I'd already typed up. The printer woke up and spit out the two-page report.

"Did you notify his emergency contact?"

"I checked his file, and there's no emergency contact listed." Larry had moved in so long ago the only items in his file were his application, a faded picture of his driver license, and a bank statement.

"That's a shame. Anything else going on I should know about?" I could hear the rustling of sheets and faint panting of a dog in the background. I imagined Patrick was in bed with his laptop open, wife asleep, canine sandwiched between them, while he finished up the month end reports for all the property owners he worked for.

Since he was obviously up and working, and since he was already on the phone, I figured it was as good a time as any to tell him about Violet. "I was at Cedar Creek tonight. Violet is missing. They found blood in her closet beneath an open window and a flooded bathroom. No body, but it doesn't look good."

"That's terrible," Patrick said so low I almost didn't hear him. "I'll have to reach out to the Dashwoods."

"Who are the Dashwoods?"

"They own the building. The husband is a surgeon, and the wife is a psychologist. They live in…Arizona, I believe. Or Alabama…I can't remember. They bought the building about ten years ago and dumped a ton of money into renovations. I've been trying to get them to use Elder Management, but they don't want a management company. If I'm not mistaken, Violet has been the manager there since the Dashwoods bought the place."

"Did they ever say anything about Violet? Like if she had murderous friends? Enemies?"

"Last time I talked to Dick—he's the husband," Patrick clarified, as if I thought Dick was the wife. Nowadays, I guess you never know. "He said she had a difficult personality."

"She was pleasant every time I spoke with her." I was on Rent or Run dot com, looking up Cedar Creek. They had a low run rate (much lower than ours) and a high ranking (almost double ours). Residents were more apt to use rating websites to rant and complain about management than to praise it, which was exactly what the last review for Cedar Creek was. "Violet is attentive, always available, and accommodating," I read out loud for Patrick. "One of the residents next door just told me that Violet was the worst manager she'd ever had."

Of course, Dolores could have been involved in Violet's disappearance, *so...there's that.*

"All I know is what Dick told me," he said. "They attempted to let her go earlier this year but were unable to because she hired a lawyer and claimed sexism, ageism, and one more ism that I can't remember."

Huh?

"And now they don't have to worry about firing her, because she is gone. Convenient."

"Don't make heavy implications like that out loud, Cambria."

"Fine." *And now they don't have to worry about firing her, because she is gone... Convenient.* "Why was Dick talking to you about Violet anyway?" I asked.

"He called last week to ask who my tax and finance guys were, and we chatted a bit. He asked me about vacancies and foot traffic. He was concerned because their vacancies sit for several months. I told him it wasn't uncommon at that price point."

"They should spend less money on things like heated toilet seats and get their rents below four grand."

"My sentiments exactly. It's a shame. If they'd let me take over that place, I could really turn a profit." He paused to daydream about all the money he'd make. "Is that boyfriend of yours on the case?"

"No." I grabbed a paper clip and began unwinding it. "His partner is, though."

Patrick hesitated. "The one with the high pants."

"Yes, and thank you." Glad I wasn't the only one who noticed.

"Bring something nice over to the staff tomorrow to pay our condolences. Make sure you say it's from me too."

"Um…sure. I can do that." It felt like an awkward gesture. Aren't you supposed to bring a condolence gift when someone has died or when they're sick? What gift do you buy in this case? Flowers? A basket of fruit?

Hi there! I heard your property manager is missing, probably dead, even if no body has been recovered. Here's a box of pears and a bouquet of hydrangeas.

No good.

Note to self: consult Google for the proper etiquette in this situation.

"Before I forget," Patrick said, his business voice back on. "I'm sending you rental increases to print and deliver tomorrow at the Burbank building."

I nearly slid out of my chair. "You want me to deliver rental increases the same day I take over?"

"It will set a good precedent."

Precedent? It sounded like an excellent way to accumulate more vacancies.

"Can we wait a couple of months?" I twisted my paper clip until it broke. "Give them time to get used to me first?" My computer pinged, and a notification appeared in the corner of my monitor. An email from Patrick with the subject line *notifications.* I clicked on the email.

Attached were rental increases for three longtime residents. Twenty dollars more a month wasn't too bad. But when it came to increases, it was less about the money and more about the principle. Residents viewed the apartments as *their* homes, and the manager as the money-hungry bad guy forcing them to pay more for *their* homes. Forgetting the manager is only doing *their* job so they can afford *their* own home.

I knew this because back in the day when I rented, I too had received a rental increase.

I too had called my manager a monster.

Not to their face, of course.

And certainly not on the internet!

"These rents are way below market value," Patrick said. "The residents know that. They'll understand."

"Most renters don't follow market trends the way you do."

"It'll be fine."

I had serious doubt everything would be *fine*, but said, "I'll make sure it is," because he was the boss and I wasn't.

What else was I supposed to do?

We hung up, and I grabbed Larry's incident report from the printer. I already had a filing cabinet filled with all the bizarre and illegal events that had transpired since I'd taken over management. I'd decided that when I retire from property management, I'd take all the reports, turn them into a novel, and make millions.

Or thousands.

Probably thousands.

So long as it was enough to cover the therapy bills.

I powered down the computer, locked the office, turned on the alarms, and took a cold shower. The water felt good against my skin, and I stayed in until my fingers pruned. I contemplated shaving my legs, told myself I'd do it tomorrow, and got out *carefully*, babying my knee. I dried off, threw on a pair of clean underwear and an oversized Lakers shirt, brushed my teeth, checked to be sure Lilly was still breathing and her window was locked, found my pepper spray, then went to bed.

Except it was too hot to sleep. I kicked the covers off and stared up at the ceiling. The fan was set to high, and the blades whirled so fast it was hard to decipher which direction they were turning. The fan reminded me of Chase. He'd installed it when I first moved in. Back when he was working undercover as the maintenance man. He was much better at solving crimes than he was at fixing things. Most of what he'd touched during his time as the maintenance man had already broken...

I set the fan to *low* and moved to the other side of the bed, so as not to be directly below it should it come crashing down. The inside temp went from manageable to suffocating, and I knew slumber was no longer an option. Instead, I thought about the man running down the stairs. His brown eyes. Long face. Prominent nose. Dark eyebrows…

Ummm…

Two ears.

One mouth…*um…*

The harder I thought, the fuzzier the memory became. I eventually fell into a fitful slumber, dreaming of Violet with her wavy brown hair swept into a claw clip, sitting on her heated toilet seat, when suddenly a bronzed man shimmied in and strangled her with a toupee.

When I woke, Lilly's little feet were kicking me in the kidneys. She must have snuck in during the night. I flipped to my stomach and buried my head into the pillow, trying for a few more minutes of sleep, but was unable to find it. My mind churned with the stairwell man, Violet, how her daughter took the news, Dolores Rocklynn in Apartment 105, Dick Dashwood, who'd tried to fire Violet a few months earlier, and…*holy hell* it was hot!

My upstairs neighbor, Mickey, jumped out of bed, thumped across the ceiling, went to the bathroom, thumped back across the ceiling, and flung himself into bed. Just as he did every freaking morning.

Whatever.

Sleep is overrated.

Lilly and I got up, got dressed, and ate breakfast. She parked herself on the couch and watched *The Little Mermaid* while I went to the office and printed the notifications and dreaded rental increases needed for the day.

The office was attached to my two-bedroom apartment. From behind my desk, I could see the lobby. We'd recently remodeled (thanks to a fire…or two). The flooring was dark wood laminate, the furniture charcoal gray with steel accents, and the walls were painted a pearl color, except for the wall behind the couch, which was orange. It was very modern LA. I loved it. Much better than the 80s drab it was before.

When I twirled in my chair, I could see my kitchen. It was the perfect setup for a single mom.

Mostly.

"Someone is here!" Lilly yelled from the living room.

I pushed against the desk and rolled backward to the door. Lilly was on the couch with her Mickey Mouse doll tucked under arm and her face glued to the television. "I didn't hear the door…"

"They knocked," she said without taking her eyes away from her show. "Me hear it."

"It's *I heard* it." Grammar is important.

I crossed the living room and checked the peephole. No one was there. I stepped outside and had a look around. *Nope.* I was about to go inside, when a hand landed on my shoulder. My fight or flight ignited. I was ninety-nine percent positive that whoever had me by the shoulder was the same person who took Violet, and I was not about to go down without a fight. I spun around and punched the intruder square in the face.

Note to self: you do have superhuman powers…oh crap.

Turned out my attacker was not an attacker at all. It was Tom.

Thomas "Tom" Dryer was my one-night-stand turned baby daddy. He was a defense attorney who represented the poor and falsely accused. He too had superhuman good looks. Tall. Very tall. Dark hair, hazel eyes, looked like a young Dylan McDermott if you squinted and turned your head to the side. My parents thought Tom was gay, but he'd slept with almost every woman this side of the equator, so I knew he wasn't. We were never a couple. I knew he had feelings for me. Maybe he even loved me in more than a she-birthed-my-kid-so-I-*have*-to-care-for-her kind of way. But commitment was his phobia, and I'd be old and gray with one foot in the grave by the time he'd be ready to settle down. So I'd resigned to peacefully co-parenting with him.

Except when I punched him in the face.

Oops.

Munch, Tom's dog, barked up at me from the ground. He had a UCLA bandana tied around his neck with a matching Bruins harness leash around his short torso. He was not happy with me.

Neither was Tom.

"Dammit, Cambria. What was that for?" Tom pinched the bridge of his nose and leaned his head back.

"Oh come on—there's no blood."

"There isn't?" Tom put his head down, and I grimaced.

"Well, yeah, OK, maybe there is. Come here." I ushered him and Munch to the kitchen table, where I placed a package of frozen peas on Tom's nose and shoved paper towels up his nostrils to stop the bleeding.

"Momma, why did you hit Daddy? 'Cause we're supposed to keep our hands to ourselves," Lilly said, pointing to the peas on Tom's face.

"That's a great rule. This was an accident, sweetie. Don't worry," I said and took a seat beside Tom. "What have I told you about scaring me like that? You're lucky I only punched you in the face."

Tom instinctually covered his manhood. "Munch ran into the bush, and I was getting him out. I wasn't trying to scare you."

"That's another thing. I've told you several times not to bring Munch here. This is a no-pet property." Also, I'm allergic to most things with fur in a can't-breathe, puffy-face, chug-the-Benadryl kind of way. Even though I adored Munch, just looking at him caused my throat to itch.

"You say that, but I see pets around here all the time."

"They're emotional pets. That's different." And a whole other issue. "What are you doing here anyway? I thought you were taking Lilly tonight."

"I was in the neighborhood...gah. This hurts." He lightly touched his nose and winced. "What's with you? Why are you so jumpy this morning?"

I scooted my chair closer and checked to be sure Lilly wasn't paying attention. "Violet, the manager next door, is missing."

Tom's eyes went round. "Since when?"

"Last night." I was interrupted when my phone buzzed. It was Amy. I held up one finger, signaling to Tom I had to take this call, and went to the kitchen, took a few breaths, and answered as cheerfully as I could. Amy and I had been best friends since the third grade. She knew me too well and could tell when something was wrong. And this was no time for her to worry about missing apartment managers. She had a tango to perfect.

Except I'm a horrible actor.

"What's wrong?" she immediately asked.

"Nothing. Nothing at all. Everything here is perfectly normal. How are you feeling? Excited? Nervous? Ready?"

"Sore!"

I pictured her sitting on the studio floor in a tank drenched with sweat. They practiced ten hours a day, seven days a week. Which sounded a lot like my own personal hell. "I called with good news. The producer said if I make it to the finale, they'll fly you out."

I slapped my hand over my mouth. "New York? Really?"

"I have to make it to the finals first, but yeah, really!"

When Amy and I were kids, we'd talk about moving to New York, where Amy would become a famous Broadway actress and I would become a nanny (what can I say? I only dream big). The pictures of Time Square and Central Park in our *Encyclopedia Britannica* were enough to spark our imaginations. Years later, we moved to Los Angeles because it was cheaper and because it was closer and because Amy wasn't coordinated enough to dance and act at the same time.

Considering Amy was a semifinalist on *Celebrity Tango* and I was an apartment manager—which is pretty much an adult nanny—I'd say we'd achieved our goals.

Mostly.

"New York, baby!" Amy sang. "And you'll get two tickets if you want to bring someone. I just need their info for the audience coordinator. They make all the arrangements ahead of time."

"When would we leave?"

"You'd leave Sunday and come back Tuesday."

That wasn't a lot of days in New York, but who was I to complain? A free vacation was exactly what I needed, and I couldn't wait to see Amy. Assuming she made the finale. However, with Raven out of the picture, I couldn't imagine her *not* making it. "I want to bring Chase. I'll send you his information. What all do you need?"

"Name, birthday, and email address. Text it to me when you get a chance. I gotta go. Kiss Lilly for me."

I said goodbye, put my phone on the counter, and did a happy dance around the kitchen.

"What's wrong with you?" Tom asked.

"If Amy makes it to the finales, I'm going to New York!" I opened the cabinet and grabbed the box of Pop-Tarts from the top shelf. "Can you watch Lilly if I get to go?"

"I guess." He removed the peas from his nose and placed the bag on the table. Hues of purple and yellow began to show beneath the skin under his eyes. Yikes. "And you're bringing *Chase*?"

"Why wouldn't I?"

Tom stood and leaned against the wall with his arms crossed and the paper towels still stuck up each nostril. "That's still going on?"

"Of course. Pop-Tart?"

"Sure."

I handed him one, folded the other in a napkin, and put it in my bag for later. "I have to get going. We can worry about the New York specifics later." I gathered my keys, files, and coloring books for Lilly, the new laptop Patrick had bought me for the Burbank office, and a bucket of cleaning supplies.

"Does Chase like *Celebrity Tango*?" Tom followed me into the office.

I checked to be sure the answering machine was on. "He likes me, and I like *Celebrity Tango*. That's what happens when you're in a relationship."

"Wouldn't you have more fun with someone else?" He followed me back into the kitchen.

I locked the office door and set the alarm. "No. I'll have more fun with my boyfriend."

"He's not really your boyfriend."

I closed the blinds. "What are you getting at? Do *you* want to go to New York and watch the finale of *Celebrity Tango*?"

"Yes. Take me instead."

"Why would I take you?"

"Because I've known Amy longer, and you and I would have more fun. If you know what I mean." He unleashed his flirty side smirk. The same one he used on me the night he knocked me up.

Oh geez.

"No," I said with conviction. "No, no, no, no, no. I am not doing this with you."

"Doing what?" He feigned obliviousness.

"I'm not doing *this* with you. This back-and-forth flirty thing you do with me. I'm not. So take your Pop-Tart, and your puppy dog eyes, and your actual dog, and go to work." I turned off the TV and sneezed into the crook of my elbow.

Tom grabbed Munch and tucked him under his arm. "I don't know what you're talking about."

"Yes, you do. I have a boyfriend. I'm very happy with him. Don't cause problems." I grabbed Lilly by the hand, walked out the front door, and waited for Tom to exit before I locked it.

Tom stopped at my side and leaned in close enough for me to smell his aftershave. "I seem to remember a pretty hot kiss in your bathroom not long ago. Does your *boyfriend* know about that?" he whispered into my ear.

Yes, I did remember.

No, my boyfriend didn't know.

You're infuriating, I mouthed to Tom so Lilly wouldn't hear.

"And you like it." He winked.

A little.

Tom grabbed the bucket of cleaning supplies for me. "All I'm saying is that I would happily go to New York. We'd have fun."

Lilly raised her hand. "Can me go too?"

I gave Tom a stop-talking-about-this-in-front-of-our-child look.

Tom heaved a sigh. "How about a piggyback ride to the car, Lil?" Tom put the bucket on the ground, swung Lilly on his back, set Munch under his arm, and Pop-Tart in hand, galloped to the parking lot.

Ugh.

My life would be a whole lot easier if he weren't so damn charming.

I grabbed my bucket, when out of the corner of my eye, I saw a man pacing in the first breezeway, and I walked over to see if he was lost.

"Can I help you?" I asked.

He pulled the knot of his tie up to look presentable, even though his suit looked as if he'd been wearing it since Christmas. Up close, his face was wrinkled and his hair wispy. "I'm looking for Daniella Lopez's apartment. Does she live here?"

"I can't say." Giving out personal information about residents is against the law.

He slipped on a pair of readers and consulted his phone. "I know she lives at this address…"

All he'd have to do was walk around the corner to see Apartment 13. Daniella had a planter box just inside her window, with *Daniella's Herbs* painted on the side. Kinda hard to miss. But I'd never seen this guy before, and if I he really did know Daniella, he'd have her apartment number.

"Are you here making a delivery or…" I left the question open-ended.

"I'd rather not say."

"You should call and let her know you're looking for her apartment."

"Or you could point me in the right direction."

"Or you could call and let her know you're looking for her."

"Tell me where she lives," he demanded.

"Sorry. I can't tell you who does and who doesn't live here. Looks like you're out of luck. The office is closed, so you'll want to exit through the pedestrian gate."

The man faltered. "I'll try later."

I followed him out to the carports. Lilly, Tom, and Munch were all waiting at my car. The man marched past them and shoved open the pedestrian gate with more force than it required.

"Who is that?" Tom asked.

"Beats me." I had my phone out, calling Daniella. It went straight to voicemail. "It's Cambria. A man I've never seen before is questioning if you live here. I can't give out personal information. Can you call me back? Thanks."

CHAPTER FOUR

———

—You have to climb your way to the top, one sperm-infested property at a time.

When you live in Los Angeles, ninety percent of your decision-making revolves around traffic. The other ten percent is dedicated to parking. The Burbank building was situated on a narrow street lined with apartment buildings, only two blocks from Warner Bros. Which meant there weren't only residents parking on the street but also those who didn't want to pay to park at the studio structure. In short, there were cars as far as my eyes could see. There were also *FOR RENT* signs as far as my eye could see. All posted on the lawns with balloons, and promises of move-in specials.

After cruising around the neighborhood, I gave up and found a spot three blocks away. It took me five minutes to figure out *if* I could actually park there, because of the street signs:

NO PARKING between the hours of 6 AM and 9 AM.

Except on Tuesdays and Thursdays.

NO PARKING on Wednesdays between the hours of 10 AM and 5 PM.

TWO HOUR PARKING ONLY Saturday and Sunday.

NO PARKING on Fridays between the hours of 7 PM and 10 PM.

It was 9:01 AM on a Tuesday. I deemed it safe and parallel parked my dented Civic between a gray Prius and a black Prius. I crawled out through the passenger door (driver's side was stuck shut and had been since it collided with a runaway dumpster). It was well over ninety degrees outside. The summer heat bounced off the street, giving a wavering illusion. I had on jeans, Converse sneakers, and a gray T-shirt I'd found in the clearance section at Target. Not exactly summer attire. I'd yet to shave my legs, so pants it was.

Fifteen minutes later, I stood in front of my newest apartment building with Lilly on my back, sweat stains under my pits, a sore knee, my bucket of cleaning supplies, and no air left in my lungs.

The extra money I got for taking the job no longer felt like enough.

This is merely a stepping stone, I reminded myself. Manage two small apartment buildings and pretty soon I'd have enough experience to apply for a large community with a full staff, thousands of units, and a golf cart to get from one end of the community to the next.

I thought about Violet. She managed a large luxurious community with a small staff. No golf cart needed, but she did drive a Mini Cooper—which is kinda the same thing. I wondered if she'd ever worked at a thirty-unit complex with peeling fascia and a seventy percent occupancy rate. I wondered if she ever had to hike three blocks with a kid on her back to get to work. I mostly wondered where she was and if she was alive. I checked my watch. It had been twelve hours since she'd disappeared, and I had serious concern about Hampton's ability to find her. At least I'd caught a glimpse of a possible suspect. That was a start. But what if Stairwell Man had nothing to do with Violet? What if Dick Dashwood, who had recently attempted to fire her, had hired someone to "take care" of her? Or Dolores, who was upset over a recent rental increase? Or what if it was none of the above? What if a random lunatic had abducted Violet? Now she's hidden somewhere. Chained up. Scared. Hurt. Or...*gasp*. Hungry?

The thought gave my stomach a roller coaster lurch.

There's no way Hampton can do this.

Not with what was happening with his wife, and dog, and best friend, and hair.

It's impossible to keep *personal* life and *professional* life completely separate. Emotions spill over, and before you know it, you're sitting at the curb outside your new place of business, talking to your boyfriend on the phone when you should be working.

Which is exactly what I was doing.

"The second story window was open. Yes, there is a fire escape, but it seems unlikely someone could go out the window with a body. Hampton needs to have the stairwell and elevator searched more closely."

"Give him a little bit more credit, Cambria. He's good at his job," Chase said at a whisper. He'd stepped out of a meeting to take my call because he's a good boyfriend like that. Also, I called multiple times until he picked up. "Last night, he told us CSI were already in the stairwell."

"*No*, he said CSI was processing the scene. He never mentioned the stairwell specifically. The crime happened less than twenty-four hours ago, and there are no police, CSI vans, detectives, crime scene tape, or search dogs to be found around the property right now! It's a ten-story building. The perp could have gone up, he could have gone down, he could have gone out the window I guess, but we just don't know. There could have been more than one person involved—"

"How do you know there's no one there now?"

"I have my resources." And my resource's name was Mrs. Nguyen. I'd called her before I called Chase and asked her to go over to Cedar Creek to see if there was any police activity. Per her report, it appeared business as usual. "Patrick said that the owners had attempted to fire Violet earlier this year. Also, Dolores is a bit suspicious. We need to investigate her more."

"We?"

"I mean *you...with my help*." Obviously.

"Have you expressed your concerns with Hampton?" Chase asked.

"I called him three times, and he didn't answer."

"Because he's working. Just because he's not at the scene doesn't mean he's not actively investigating. Please, let him do his job, and don't insert yourself into the middle of the...*wait*. Don't you start at Burbank this morning?"

Oh. Right. That.

"Um...yes."

"You're not going to let this go, are you?" Chase asked, still in a whisper.

Not a chance. But for now, "I do need to get back to work. Call me tonight?"

"Be careful."

"I always am."

Mostly.

I hung up the phone and stretched my lower back, twisting from side to side, and rolled my neck. It was hard to go about business as usual when there was a giant question mark over Violet's whereabouts. But the building wasn't going to manage itself, and I still had bills to pay, owners to please, and a job to keep.

Lilly skipped ahead, and I grabbed my bucket, gave myself a five-second pep talk, and it was go-time.

The Burbank building was a two-story Spanish style with clean landscaping and a towering palm tree in the front. There was no security gate. Lilly and I walked under an archway, past the mailboxes, into the courtyard, and found my office door. It was labeled *Storage Closet* because that was exactly what it was: a storage closet. The previous manager didn't spend more than a few hours a week there. No need for an office. If I wanted to rent apartments, then I had to be available to show vacant units. If I had to be there, then I had to have a clean place for my kid to play, because no matter how much of an increase in pay I got, it still wasn't enough to cover full-time childcare.

The storage closet door was warped, splintery, and swollen shut. I used my shoulder and hip to push it open and…*aaaahhhhhhhh!*

Two teenagers were behind a power washer, having sex. Sex!

I jumped back and bumped into a shelving rack. A box of outlet covers fell on my head.

"Hey! A little privacy," the boy said. He had a squeaky voice, barely there facial hair, and a tattoo on his leg—of what? I didn't care to examine. All I knew for sure was, he used his free hand to shoo me away.

He shooed *me* away.

"Don't you shoo me away, young man." I felt very much like a crotchety old grandma, wagging my finger at the two. "I'm the manager, so you *shoo* before I call the police."

It took a second for the news to sink into their minds. Once grasped, they scrambled to their feet, zipping, buttoning, and refastening all articles of clothing.

I stepped out of their way as they rushed out the door, and my foot knocked over an unopened box of condoms.

You've got to be kidding me!

I leaned out the doorway with the box of condoms high above my head, like I was the Statue of Lifestyles Ultra Thin Liberty, about to go all *After School Special* on them, but a gorgeous specimen of a man stood in front of me, and I forgot what was happening.

Errr...

"I'm looking for the manager," the guy said with a smolder. He was probably early twenties with high cheekbones, pouty lips, dark skin, and blue eyes.

"Her's the manager." Lilly cocked her thumb in my direction.

"Yes...yes her is." I ventured a smile and tossed the condoms through the open door. The box hit the frame, fell to the ground, and rolled between us.

"Are those balloons?" Lilly asked.

"Um..." I kicked the box inside the storage closet and closed the door. "I'm...*hi*. How can I help you?"

"The name is Fox. I saw the *For Rent* sign on the lawn. Do you have any studios?"

"Why yes. Yes! We do have a studio apartment. Yes." I pulled at the collar of my shirt, suddenly remembering the sweat stains circling under my pits and, I assumed, on my back from where I'd carried Lilly. Not that super-hot Fox would be interested in *me*. Not that I was in a position to be interested in *him*.

"When were you looking to move in?" I asked him, playing it cool. If sounding like you just took your mouth out of a helium spout was considered cool.

"Immediately. I can't commit to anything long term though." He ran his hand along the ridges of his abdomen, which were visible through his sheer white shirt. "I need a month-to-month. In case the ladies figure out where I live."

"Come again?"

"You know how chicks are." He pulled up the bottom of his shirt to reveal his washboard.

Hot *and* arrogant.

Like ketchup on a banana. Cheese Whiz on Frosted Flakes. Pineapple on pizza…all gross combinations.

Sexual fantasy officially over.

Arrogant or not, he was still a prospective resident, and I had vacancies to fill. I took him to the second floor to the only rent-ready studio available.

I peeked my head in first to be sure no one was naked in there too, saw the coast was clear, and let Fox in. The studio was much like the studio apartments at my LA building. It was a room with a kitchen, and it cost 1,700 dollars a month.

Fox ran his finger along the windowsill and inspected the two kitchen cabinets. "Come with parking?" he asked.

"No."

"Laundry?"

"No."

"Air conditioning?"

"No."

"Is the place gluten-free?"

"Come again?"

"Is this apartment gluten-free?" he repeated, slower this time.

"I don't know," I said.

"I'm off all dairy, soy, gluten, meat, rice, and casein."

"Then what do you eat?"

"Eggs."

"Eggs. Right." I blew out a breath. "I'm assuming the place is gluten-free, but I can double-check with my maintenance supervisor."

"If it is, then I'll take it. When should I move in?"

"You'll first need to fill out an application. Once you're approved and put down a deposit, you can move in immediately."

Fox chuckled. The smolder returned. "Do you honestly need me to fill out an application?"

"It's company policy."

"Come on. You know who I am."

"You're Fox," Lilly said.

"Don't pretend you don't recognize me. I just did a spread in the *Los Angeles Real Estate Magazine*. Watch." Fox put one hand on his hip and held out his other arm, making a cup with his hand. "Look familiar?"

"You're a little teapot!" Lilly clapped her hands. "I can do it, too." She struck a teapot pose.

Fox dropped his arms. "No. Imagine I'm holding a drill." He resumed his pose.

Lilly and I exchanged a look. You know you're weird when a three-year-old thinks so. "I'll be on the lookout," I said. "Let's get you that application."

The three of us went back to my office, and I grabbed the paperwork from my bag. I went over the instructions, and Fox promised to return shortly with the application and the fee.

Then it was time to de-germ my "office." I gave Lilly my phone and a coloring book to keep her occupied, snapped on a pair of gloves, grabbed my bottle of bleach, and got to work.

Two hours of scrubbing, sterilizing, gagging, and dumping trash that had been there at least a decade, and my office was ready. Sure it was small. Enough room for a desk—as soon as I bought one. No window, which was a bummer since there was also no ventilation. But it was specimen free, and that was all I had the energy to care about.

Fox dropped off his application and the fee. I scanned the information to be sure everything was filled out. Looked good. Pending his rental and job verifications went well and the apartment was gluten-free, I suspected he'd be in by the weekend.

Half a day on the job, and I'd rented an apartment.

I was pleased with my managing skills.

Lilly was not.

She was hot, and tired, and hungry, and bored, and three. Tears spilled out of her hazel eyes and down her rosy cheeks as she gasped for air between sobs. I tried to console her, and she pushed me away. I tried to offer an alternative activity. "Why don't you draw a picture for Mrs. Nguyen? She'll love that." Lilly threw the box of crayons at my nose and berated me in Vietnamese. I tried to explain to her that her actions were not OK and that Mommy had to work and if I didn't work, then we wouldn't have a home, or food, or clothes, or toys. She didn't care. She didn't care one bit.

Frantic, I dug through my purse in search of a bribe. "What about a mint?"

"No!"

"A granola bar?"

"No!"

"Fish crackers?"

"No!"

"How about *one...ten...twenty...*forty-two cents?"

"No!"

"A red marker? A Target receipt? ChapStick? My credit card?" I'd buy her a freaking Mercedes if she would just stop screaming.

OK, maybe not a Mercedes, more like a used Kia.

Nothing worked.

"Let's go!" She threw herself on the ground outside.

The hypochondriac in me thought about all the different strands of influenza she was currently rolling around in. The mom in me was about to lose it. The apartment manager in me was concerned about the noise level. Her high-pitched screams echoed through the community—maybe even all of Burbank. Hell, the crews of the International Space Station were probably hunched over in agony with their fingers in their ears.

"Lilly, I understand that you're upset, but I—"

"Let's go!"

"We will. Right now we have to—"

"I hate this place." She kicked the wall. "I want my daddy!"

Ouch.

I crouched beside her and tucked a curl behind her ear. "You can see Daddy soon."

The promise of reuniting with Tom calmed her. She took a shaky breath and wiped the tears from her eyes.

Double ouch.

"Let me finish one last thing, and we'll leave."

She gave a feeble nod of her little head.

Note to self: find affordable preschool, ASAP.

Luckily, there was only one item left on my to-do list.

Unluckily, that was to pass out a *Three-Day Notice to Cure* to every single resident who lived there. Each apartment had at least one lease violation, whether it be the wet towels slung over the patio, the ashtray in the walkway, dead plant by the door, or old cardboard covering the window. It was obvious these residents had been without an apartment manager for awhile. Or the previous manager didn't care.

I was incapable of not caring.

My eye twitched just looking at the bag of trash by Apartment 6A's door, thinking of all the insects and rodents lurking, waiting to dig in.

Gross.

There were also the rental increase notices I had to pass out. Each one sealed in an envelope with the Elder Management logo on the flap. My original plan was to go door-to-door, introduce myself, point out the lease violation, kindly ask the resident to rectify the problem, and hand deliver those who were getting increases.

Except Lilly was moments from another meltdown and we still had to stop by the police station so I could meet with a sketch artist in…I checked my watch. *Crap.* Thirty minutes.

There was no time for pleasantries.

It was for the better, I told myself. I was pleasant and overly accommodating when I started at the LA building, and residents still trampled all over me.

Example: Last month, Daniella from Apartment 13 placed a cup of live crickets on the counter and told me to feed them to Gary (her tarantula) for the next two weeks while she visited her cousin in Miami. She didn't ask me. She *told* me. And I said, "Sure," because I have boundary issues.

In Burbank I was not Pushover Cambria. I was Stern Cambria! And I would run this circus with an iron fist.

Mostly!

Also, I was in a rush.

I stuck the *Three-Day Notice to Cure* outlining the infractions onto each door, placed the rental increases in the respective mailboxes, grabbed my stuff, and ran away as fast as I could before Lilly screamed. A fifteen-minute trek to my car. Five-minute break to catch my breath. A crying toddler strapped in her car seat. And we were off.

The guilt of dropping the notifications and bailing began to fester as I drove away. Especially since I had no plans to return until Thursday, giving residents twenty-four hours to fester in their anger. Which didn't seem like a good idea, and I couldn't help but think about the fact that Violet gave out rental increases and twenty-four hours later she was gone.

CHAPTER FIVE

———

—It's impossible to parent full-time and work full-time at the same exact time without losing your mind.

It took twenty minutes to drive to the police station, which wouldn't have been a problem except Lilly fell asleep five minutes before we arrived.

A few things I'd learned as a mother.

One: Never wear white. It doesn't end well.

Two: Never interrupt toddlers who are playing quietly on their own. It doesn't end well.

Three: Never, ever, ever, under any circumstance, ever, ever, *ever* wake a child from an unplanned nap.

Unless you have an appointment with a forensic sketch artist and you're already late.

I stood at the counter in the lobby of the police station. The officer behind the Plexiglas had given up competing with Lilly. Who screamed as if her life depended on it. I held her tight as she thrashed and kicked and fought to break free. Every single pore in my body pumped out sweat as if *my* life depended on it.

I was not about to put Lilly on the floor of a dirty police station.

I was, however, about to sell her on eBay. Especially once she began screaming at me in Vietnamese.

"You need to stop, Lilly," I said through gritted teeth, struggling to keep my composure. The woman standing one window over—who had a leopard print leotard on, no shoes, hair the size of Canada, and a ferret on a leash—cast her judgy eyes in my direction and shook her head. Which did nothing to help the situation.

"I'm supposed...to meet...with a forensic...sketch artist," I huffed. Lilly somehow managed to turn upside down. I had her by the waist, and her little legs flailed around like they were two inflatable tube men summoning passersby to her used car lot. "My...name...is Cambria Clyne. Detective Hampton...sent me."

Note to self: find an all-day preschool today.

We were finally escorted through the secured doors and taken down a long hallway, past offices and officers and grim-looking individuals who looked to have recently sobered up. I followed my escorting officer to a corner desk tucked behind a partition. My eyes were instantly drawn to the sketches pinned to the walls. Men and women, some with mug shots beside them, some with *CAUGHT* stamped across the top in red ink. Some individuals looked scary, some were smiling, and others had defining features like a mole or a scar. Apprehension thunked into my gut. I tried to summon the picture of the brown-eyed man back to my head, except Lilly was kicking me in the head, and I was having a hard time activating my temporal lobe.

The sketch artist stood and greeted us with a warm smile and motioned for me to take a seat in the chair beside his desk. "Thank you for coming down, Ms. Clyne. I'm Calvin. And who is this?" Calvin was about my age, with a pompadour haircut.

"This is Lilly," I answered for her since she was currently upside down and crying.

Calvin rolled his chair closer. "Lilly, who is your favorite Disney princess?"

Lilly stared at the man as if he were contagious.

"She's into *The Little Mermaid* right now," I said and wrestled Lilly into a sitting-up position. She tucked her head into my chest and rubbed her eyes.

"*The Little Mermaid* is one of my favorites." Calvin tapped one of two computer screens on his desk, grabbed a stylus from a penholder, and began to draw. His hand moved with such fluidity that both Lilly and I were memorized. With a click of the mouse, the printer below his desk spit out a picture of Ariel with Lilly's name on the top.

Her little face lit up. She grabbed the paper and examined it, wiping tears from her cheeks.

I wanted to give Calvin a hug.

So I did.

"Thank you," I said. "I'm so sorry. I had to wake her from a nap."

"No need to apologize. My daughter gets the same way," he said.

I took a breath for what felt like the first time since I entered the building.

"My grandpa's name is Calvin," Lilly said with a sniffle.

"Is that right? And his last name is *Clyne?*" He looked to me for confirmation.

"It is. He's a plumber in Fresno, and his business is called Calvin Clyne Plumbing. Made high school real fun."

"I bet," Calvin said with a snort and rolled his chair back to his desk. "Let's go ahead and get started. Can you give me a general description of this man's face shape and features?"

Er...

I told him what I could remember, which still wasn't much. Calvin asked if the man had a doppelgänger, but I failed to think of one. He asked if the man had any distinguishing features, but I failed to think of one.

Per the usual, I was a big help.

Calvin next pulled an album from behind his desk and showed me pictures of lips, noses, eyebrows, and hairlines. I flipped through the book. Nothing looked familiar. Had I known I would have to decipher whether this man had full lips or thin lips, how bushy his brows were, or if he had forehead wrinkles, I would have paid more attention during the five seconds we'd interacted.

As it was, the entire thing felt like a hopeless waste of Calvin's time. If he felt the same, he didn't show it. He remained patient; his stylus danced around the computer screen as he added a wrinkle, and then took it away when I wasn't sure. It was an hour of adding and erasing features until Calvin turned the screen, and I let out a gasp.

Holy crap!

CHAPTER SIX

———

—I am not authorized.

The sketch looked exactly like a young Bob Saget and, yet, also exactly like Stairwell Man. Which made me feel better. Danny Tanner wouldn't kill anyone.

Of course, his doppelgänger might.

I snapped a picture of the sketch with my phone, and it was time to go home.

Well, almost.

First, we had to stop at County Hospital.

Out of the way, yes, but I wanted to check on Larry.

I found a parking spot on the street and made sure each door was locked. Not that anyone would see my dented Civic with the taped side mirror, ripped seats, missing hubcaps, broken driver's-side door, and think, *I bet we could strip this for parts!* But I had a buck fifty in the cup holder—enough to buy a bean and cheese burrito from Taco Bell.

County Hospital wasn't exactly located in the good side of town. Hence the metal detectors and bag search performed upon arrival. Lilly and I were given a visitor's sticker and followed the signs to the information desk, where a nurse wearing blue scrubs and a pink hijab was working. Per her name tag, this was Laylaa.

Laylaa welcomed us with a full-face smile. "Can I help you?"

"We're here to visit a friend who was brought in last night via ambulance," I said.

"Go ahead and sign in here." She handed me a clipboard, and I jotted down our names and whom we were visiting and handed it back to her.

"I'm not sure what room he is in though."

"Not a problem. Let me check for you." Laylaa consulted the clipboard and rolled her chair over to the computer.

I propped an elbow on the counter and had a look around. Hospitals made me anxious. The sterile smell. The sound of rubber-soled shoes on the hard floor. The wheelchairs. The paging system. All the germs floating in the air...*ugh.* I stuck my hand under the automatic antibacterial dispenser and gave Lilly a Purell bath.

"Please wait. I need to make a call," Laylaa said. She spun around in her chair and picked up the phone. No matter how hard I tried (and I tried *really* hard), I couldn't overhear the conversation.

"I'm sorry," she said after she hung up. "Your friend is not allowed visitors at this time."

I blinked. "Larry loves visitors. What do you mean he's not allowed?"

Laylaa clasped her hands. "I'm sorry. No visitors allowed at this time."

I gasped. Oh no. "Is he...is he..." I leaned over the desk and whispered, "D-e-a-d?"

"I'm not permitted to give away patient information, but I can assure you he's being taken care of."

What a weird comment. "But he's not *allowed* to have visitors."

"Correct," Laylaa said, unmoving.

"Is he in the ICU? Because I'm not sure he has any family around or anyone to be with him."

Laylaa's brown eyes moved to the side and back again. I turned to see what had caught her attention. A security guard who looked like he could be the starting center for the Los Angeles Lakers stepped forward and peered down at me like I was lunch. *Gulp.* "Is there a problem here?" he asked.

I took a step in front of Lilly. "No problem. We came to visit a friend—that's all." I turned to Laylaa. "Would you allow me to speak to a doctor?"

"Not at this time."

"But if he were in critical condition, you'd notify someone, right?"

"Of course we would," she said. "But your friend is not allowed unauthorized visits at this time."

"Unauthorized? He's not the president of the United States. He's a...he's a..." *A what?* It dawned on me that I had no idea what Larry did for a living. He seemed always to be home, and he'd written *self-employed* on his application when he'd moved in. "How do you become authorized?"

"I'm sorry. I think it's best you leave now," Laylaa said.

I was so confused. I'd visited lots of people in the hospital before. Well, not *lots*. Mainly my Grandma Ruthie toward the end of her life. Even if Grandma wasn't up for visitors, the nurse would simply say, "She's not up for visitors right now." There was no talk of authorization. This was County Hospital! Roughly a bazillion people were wheeled through those doors daily. Did everyone have to be authorized to visit?

A woman with a baby strapped to her chest pushed past me and leaned over the desk to speak to Laylaa. "I'm here to see Donner Spanster. Can you give me his room number please?"

Laylaa consulted her computer. "He's in room 1245 on the third floor. Please sign your name here."

What?

I should have dropped it and left.

But I couldn't. I pictured Larry lying in a hospital bed all alone.

"Could you please let Larry know that I'm here," I said to Laylaa.

She sighed. The same I'm-just-doing-my-job type of sigh that I'd sighed many times myself.

"Go home now," the guard said.

Geez.

Lilly's head was buried into the back of my leg, and I could tell the exchange made her uncomfortable. So we left. What else was I to do? I wasn't authorized.

Whatever that meant.

CHAPTER SEVEN

———

—Fruit is expensive.

My Grandma Ruthie used to say, "When you can't make sense of what's happening, call Mom."

So I did.

"They escorted you out?" Mom sounded as confused as I felt.

I checked the rearview mirror. I was still parked by the hospital, and Lilly was asleep in her car seat, finishing the nap she'd started earlier. I dared not wake her this time. "We weren't exactly escorted out. The nurse said he wasn't *allowed* unauthorized visitors, and a security guard told me to go home."

"Do they have a no-children policy?"

"A woman came in with a baby right after me, and why wouldn't they just say no children allowed?"

"I don't know. People are rude these days." Mom paused to bark orders to someone in the background. She worked as a secretary at a busy meat-packing company in Fresno—and had since my parents divorced two decades ago. "I don't think it's uncommon for a patient to ask for no visitors. Especially if they're in a lot of pain or very sick. But the whole unauthorized business sounds weird to me. Is he on police watch?"

"No. All he did was fall from..." *Crap.* I thought about what Kevin had said to the dispatch operator, about Larry being armed. Could the police have taken Kevin seriously and put Larry on a twenty-four-hour hold.

Dang it, Kevin.

"What's wrong, Cambria?"

"Nothing. I just…remembered that I have a thing to do. I've gotta go." I wasn't about to tell my mom about what Kevin had said, because then I'd have to explain who Kevin was. Which could lead to a conversation about other areas of my life, like Chase, and my very un-gay baby daddy, and that one time someone tried to kill me, and the other time someone tried to kill me, and there was the incident with the drug dealers. It was best to keep my parents in the dark. For their own sanity.

And mine.

"I can tell something else is wrong." Mom's hobbies included studying the fluctuation of my voice. "Is it a boy?"

Technically yes, but "No."

I could feel my mother's disappointment radiating through the phone. "You know what? It's fine." She cleared her throat, and I pictured her smoothing back her Einstein-ish blonde hair. "Being a powerful single woman is in nowadays. You should consider a sperm donor."

I just about choked on my own spit. How had *sperm* come into the conversation? I looked down at my phone to be sure I was still connected with *my* mother. She'd about had a heart attack when I'd told her I was pregnant with Lilly. Of course, that had more to do with me being unmarried, financially unstable, and living in an apartment I'd dubbed Crap-o-La. "Are *you* OK, Mom? Since when did you want me to have more children?"

"I've been thinking a lot lately. Your father and I were kids when we had you, and we had no idea what we were doing. The thought of having another child was too overwhelming at the time. But I can't help but wonder if you had a sibling, then maybe you wouldn't be so eager to insert yourself into other people's lives."

"Excuse me?"

"Cambria. You have this unhealthy need to fix things. Most landlords wouldn't go through so much trouble to visit a tenant in the hospital. They'd send flowers. If that. It's not part of your job. I wonder if you'd had a younger sibling to care for, then you wouldn't be in this situation and you'd have healthier boundaries. I'm only thinking of Lilly."

Oh geez. "Are you watching Dr. Phil again?"

"No. I'm listening to his podcast. Cambria, you really should listen to it too. You're way too young and far too pretty, with way too much potential to be working a thankless job."

I applied my forehead to the steering wheel. "I'll keep that in mind."

"You're welcome," she said, even though I hadn't thanked her. "I'm here to help."

I could hear the smile in her voice. Nothing pleased her more than when I'd call for help, which I'd done exactly three times.

One: during my first—and only year—of college, when I couldn't figure out how to make the iron steam.

Two: right after Lilly was born. I'd stepped on a thumbtack and couldn't remember if I'd ever had a tetanus shot.

Three: twenty minutes earlier when I called to ask about the hospital.

I didn't have a thankless job...OK, maybe I did. But I had Amy. She was basically my sister!

I turned around to check on Lilly. Drool slithered down her chin, and she flinched in her sleep. A pang of guilt stabbed my heart. She was nearly four years old and spent a majority of her time around adults. No siblings in the near future.

This is why I don't call Mom.

She'd make me feel guilty and think too hard. And I didn't have time to think. Not with a boyfriend on a special assignment, residents falling from the roof, and apartment managers disappearing.

Still, she made a point.

Then I remembered Violet's daughter. She'd grown up without siblings and in the property management world. Now she lived in a big house with her husband, two kids, and a great job.

There was still hope.

After I hung up with my mom, Lilly happily woke on her own. We stopped at the mall to buy a gift for the Cedar Creek staff. I couldn't decide between a bouquet of flowers or a fruit basket, and Google was of no help. So I bought a bouquet of fruit. I took it a step above and paid extra for chocolate-dipped fruit.

Because I'm classy like that.

And Patrick was paying for it.

When I got home, Kevin was waiting by my door. He had on twill coveralls and bare feet. He took classes at the local junior college at night and worked for a cleaning company during the day. "The only job worse than yours," he'd said when he started. Kevin had only just entered the *real world*. Twenty years ago, his parents had given him the boot when they'd found out he was gay. They'd sent him there to live rent-free so long as he didn't contact them. The arrangement was going well until Kevin was arrested on charges of cocaine possession and checked himself out of rehab. Then it was decided by the family trustee that he should start paying rent.

It had been a hard adjustment.

For all of us.

Kevin's face skewed up into a question mark. "What is that?"

"It's a chocolate-dipped fruit bouquet." I dug my keys out of my bag and unlocked the door.

"Why do you have it?" Kevin followed me inside and closed the door behind him. Lilly ran off to her bedroom, and I dropped my bag and the fruit on the kitchen counter.

"It's for the Cedar Creek staff," I said.

Kevin's face went blank.

"Because of Violet," I tried.

Still nothing.

"The apartment manager. Violet Pumpkin. She went missing last night."

"So you bought them fruit on a stick to make them feel better?"

"It's *chocolate*-dipped fruit on a stick."

"How much does something like that cost?"

"Not important." Seventy-five bucks.

"Looks a little lopsided."

"I got hungry. It's been a long day." I took a seat at the table and dropped my chin into my palm. "Motherhood is kicking my butt. Oh, by the way. I stopped to see Larry at the hospital. I think your comment about him being armed caused a problem. They're not allowing him to have visitors."

Kevin shrugged me off and opened the fridge. He took out a yogurt and peeled off the lid. "So what. He probably doesn't want people showing up in his room."

"They didn't say not taking visitors. She was quite specific. He's not *allowed* visitors right now. All I know is that Larry runs into the office when he has a suspicious mole. There's no doubt in my mind that he would like visitors when in the hospital. You need to tell the police that you lied."

"I can't say that, because we don't know if he was armed."

"Kevin! He wasn't armed. You need to get over this rift you have with him. Isn't forgiveness a recovery step?"

Kevin licked the excess yogurt off the lid and tossed it in the trash "Why don't you go deliver your lopsided fruit basket and leave my recovery steps alone."

"Fine. But you need to tell the police you were wrong." I grabbed the fruit and called down the hallway. "Lilly, I'm going next door. Do you want to stay with Kevin or come with me?"

"I want to go." Lilly appeared in a Cinderella dress with plastic slip-on heels.

Um...

Whatever.

At least she was clothed and not screaming.

* * *

All seemed normal at Cedar Creek. The police cars and CSI trucks were gone. I remembered the step and saved myself from taking another tumble onto the scorching cement. I debated using the code Dolores had given me, but decided to use the intercom instead. I pressed 0 for the leasing office and waited.

"Come in," came a woman's voice. She didn't even ask who it was. Which struck me as odd, given the manager had been abducted less than twenty-four hours earlier. If it were me, I'd be more picky about whom I allowed in.

There was a *ping* followed by a *click*, and I pushed open the whimsical door and walked directly into a freezer. Holy crap. The A/C had to be on full blast.

The drastic change in body temp caused a shiver to crawl down my spine and bumps to erupt on my arms. I could practically see my breath.

In the office sat a woman with short, spiky light blonde hair. Per the plaque proudly displayed on her desk, this was the assistant manager.

Lilly and I stood at the entryway, but the assistant manager didn't notice us. She was too busy fussing around and muttering to herself.

"Knock, knock," I said, not wanting to touch the glass door.

"Hello. Can I help you?" she said through a businesslike smile that faded. "Cambria! Come in. Come in." The woman hurried around the desk and moved the pile of papers on the chair.

I took a seat with the fruit on my lap and Lilly clinging to my side.

"And you sweet thing, what's your name?" The manager bent down to address Lilly. She had a nasally basso voice and a rough cackle. It reminded me a little of Joyce, the previous manager whom I'd taken over for. Except Joyce was about seventy pounds wet and a chain smoker. The assistant manager was younger, and rounder, and her voice was deeper and…OK, she was nothing like Joyce.

Lilly didn't answer. Instead, she stuck her fingers in her mouth.

"Her name is Lilly," I said.

"Lilly!" The assistant manager cackled. "That is my favorite flower. Do you want to see our kids' corner?"

Lilly looked to me for approval.

"Go for it," I said.

"It's right over there." The assistant manager pointed to a child's table with crayons, paper, and a small dollhouse in the corner of the lobby. A marvelous idea.

Got me thinking: if I had a kids' corner, then I'd rent to people who actually had kids, specifically three- to four-year-old girls. They'd be friends with Lilly, and I wouldn't feel guilted into procreation.

Note to self: invest in a kids' corner.

Lilly shuffled over with her heels clanking across the floor to the kids' corner and picked a coloring book. The assistant manager sat down, and it dawned on me that, even though she knew my name, I didn't know hers.

"I'm sorry," I said. "Have we met before?" Surely I'd remember meeting her. Unlike my Bob Saget look-a-like, Assistant Manager had unforgettable features. Like the mole on her right cheek. The blue eye shadow that covered the entire surface area between her lashes and the highest point of her brows. Eyebrows that were penciled in and started at the inner corner of her eyes and arched over to the outer corners. Like a McDonald's logo on her forehead. Her lipstick was bright red, and her teeth were coffee stained.

"My goodness." She took a handheld electric fan from the top drawer of her desk and switched it on. "I'm sorry for my bad manners. No, we haven't formally been introduced. My name is Stormy Albright. I'd shake your hand, but I'm drenched. Damn hot flashes. Just you wait."

I had to concentrate to keep my teeth from chattering. "I came over to bring you this." I held up the fruit. "It's from Elder Management."

"That's so sweet of you. I haven't had a thing to eat all day. It's been nutty coo-coo crazy here."

"I bet. I'm so sorry about Violet. Have you heard anything new?"

Stormy grabbed the fruit bouquet, pulled a dipped pineapple from the stack, and picked off the chocolate. "I'm telling everyone that she went on a vacation, because you know how rumors fly. Truth is, I haven't heard a thing. The woman never takes a day off." Stormy put the chocolate into her mouth and tossed the pineapple into the trash.

"Have you spoken with Detective Hampton?"

"He came over to my apartment last night. At first I was excited when I checked my peephole and saw a man on the other side. Men don't just show up on your doorstep when you reach my age. Just you wait."

I assumed Stormy was in her mid to late forties. About the same age as my mother. Too young to be talking so old.

Granted, I sucked at age guesstimating.

"Then he flashed his badge, and I just about tossed my cookie," Stormy continued. "Poor Violet. Bless her heart. He told me they suspected *foul play*." She mouthed the last part, as if afraid to say the words out loud. "I told him I didn't know anyone who would want to hurt Violet but..." She looked over her shoulder to be sure no one was listening and leaned in closer. I scooted to the end of my chair and placed my elbows on the desk. When Stormy spoke, she did so at a whisper. "For the last few months, Violet has been acting strange."

"How so?" I whispered back.

"I caught her eating a Twinkie."

"A Twinkie," I said in horror, even though I'd had one for lunch.

"Yes, a Twinkie. I never saw the woman eat anything that wasn't green."

So Violet was one of those non-processed food people. I had no idea.

"She was so jumpy," Stormy went on. "Agitated all the time. I think she was losing it a bit." She tapped her temple.

"Why do you think she was agitated?" I suspected it was because she'd almost been fired, but I didn't want to mention the *F* word in front of Violet's subordinate in case she didn't know.

"I think it has something to do with the owners." She plucked a chocolate-dipped strawberry from the bouquet, peeled the chocolate off, and trashed the berry. "They don't get along very well. Violet says Mr. Dashwood's mother must have had a premonition when she named him."

I don't...oh! I got it.

Dick Dashwood.

Ha!

"Do you know why they didn't get along?" I asked.

"Violet has a...*strong* personality. She likes things her way. Doesn't want to be questioned. Doesn't like to answer to anyone. She told me the owners should butt out and let her run the place as she sees fit. I honestly think the owners are scared of her because they *never* come around."

Huh?

I wondered if Hampton had talked to the Dashwoods yet.

"This whole thing gives me a big fat headache," Stormy said with a sigh. "I came to Los Angeles to be an actress, not to manage apartments. This whole business is whackadoodle. I've worked here three years and don't know much about Violet. She mostly keeps to herself and does her job, and I keep to myself and do mine. Except..." She grabbed three tissues and dabbed her glistening décolleté. "I don't even know how to work this thing." She poked at the keyboard with her finger like it might bite. "Let alone work the management software program. Violet said there was no point in my learning to use it."

"But you're the assistant manager?"

"Violet liked to handle all the leases, rent collection, management, and...mostly everything herself."

That's unfortunate. If I had an assistant manager, I'd have him handle all the leases, and filing, and market surveys...it would be glorious. A girl could only dream. "One trick I've learned is you can find a tutorial for almost anything on YouTube."

Stormy peeled a Post-it from a stack by the phone and grabbed a pen. "You Tube. Is that one word or two?"

I stared at her and blinked. "It's one word. Spelled y-o-u-t-u-b-e."

"And I find that on the internet?"

"Um...*yes.*"

Stormy stuck the yellow Post-it on the perimeter of her computer screen. She had barely legible chicken scratch handwriting. "This is helpful. I haven't heard from the owners yet, but I suspect it's now my job to keep this place afloat." There was nothing but trepidation in her voice.

"I'm sure you'll be fine." I tried to sound more optimistic than I felt. If she had no idea how to use YouTube, then she was screwed. I knew from experience that keeping a place afloat was a lot harder than one would think. "If there's anything I can do, please let me know. I'm very worried about Violet, and I realize how crucial the next day and a half is."

Stormy ripped another sticky note from the stack. "Write down your cell on here for me."

"Um...sure." I grabbed a pen and jotted down my number. "Also, before I forget, when I was here last night, I saw a man in the stairwell running from, I assume, Violet's apartment. I went to the police station and met with a sketch artist." I pulled out my phone. "Have the police showed you this?" I turned my screen to show her the picture of Bob Saget Stairwell Man.

She studied the picture. "I don't recognize him."

"Have you spoken with Antonio?" I rubbed my hands together to get warm. "How's he doing?"

"He's doing alright, I think." She shrugged her shoulders. "We don't talk much. He mostly dealt with Violet."

"How's Dolores doing in Apartment 105? I heard there was quite a bit of damage in her apartment."

"Mostly just the ceiling. Antonio is taking care of it."

"Did a plumber ever come out?" I asked casually.

Stormy shrugged. "Dunno."

She was really of no help.

I heard the clanking of Lilly's heels on the floor and felt a tug on my shirt. "Looks what me made." She held up a picture of Winnie-the-Pooh colored in purple and pink.

"It's beautiful. Are you ready to go?"

She nodded.

I stood and grabbed Lilly by the hand. "Again, I'm so sorry about Violet."

"Let's hope this is one big misunderstanding and Violet shows up tomorrow. Home from a wild Vegas trip with a big hangover."

I agreed, that would be nice. Highly unlikely, but nice.

Who goes to Vegas without their wallet and cell phone?

Lilly and I said goodbye and stepped into the lobby. Stormy returned to fussing around her desk, eating the chocolate off the fruit, and paid no attention to us. Good, because I wanted to check out the stairwell, and I didn't want to pester her. I remembered how stressful it was to receive on-the-job training from a YouTube video.

I swung Lilly onto my hip and quickly scooted down the hallway, past Apartment 105, and past a man hauling skis to his apartment, and past a woman walking her cat (*ah-choo!*), and past the elevator, and past the mailman, and to the stairwell. I pushed open the door and looked up. The staircase spiraled up ten stories.

"What we doing in here?" Lilly asked and her voice echoed.

"I want to look at one thing before we leave." I shifted her to my back and checked the surroundings more thoroughly.

There was a triangle opening under the first story stairwell, the perfect place to hide if you were, gee, I don't know, a murderer waiting to strike your next victim? Except all I found was ten cents, a dolly, a rusting bucket of white paint, an *Out of Order* sign, and about ninety-five pieces of discarded gum. Lilly reached out her little finger and touched one before I could stop her. I screamed. She screamed. I cried. She cried. I gagged. She laughed. I bathed her in Purell. WebMD said she'd be fine. And we continued.

There was nothing suspicious.

But since I was already in the building, and since I was already in the stairwell, and since Lilly was behaving so well and was freshly de-germed, I went upstairs to Violet's apartment.

The door was closed and locked with no sign stating this was an active crime scene. Anyone with a key could easily enter and do as they please! Even I knew that a crime scene must be secured—and I received all my CSI knowledge from, well, *CSI*!

Honestly.

I checked the floor in the hallway, not exactly sure what I was looking for, but I found a quarter and a smudge that resembled a tire mark near the baseboard next to the elevator. It could mean nothing. Or it could mean everything. I supposed the perp could have taken the elevator. Stairs would have made for a faster getaway. But not everyone has elevator aversions like I do. I snapped a picture of the smudge and sent it to Hampton.

Now thirty-five cents richer, I decided there was nothing more to do and it was time to go. With Lilly still on my back, we managed to get through the lobby unnoticed, and we stepped into the 102 degree summer day. We said hello to the koi fish swimming in the pond and watched the light dance across their scales.

"Can me go swimming today?" Lilly asked.

"It's *I*, and that's a wonderful idea." I smiled, happy to see her in a better mood.

Very happy.

I put her on the ground, and we strolled hand-in-hand down the walkway. My heart felt heavy, thinking about Violet, and about Stormy, frantically picking up the pieces in Violet's absence. I couldn't help but think about who would step in if I disappeared tomorrow. Would someone be able to sit at my desk and pick up where I left off? Would they know you had to jiggle the storage room lock to get it to open? That I let Sophia from Apartment 38 clean the laundry rooms for extra cash? Or that Mickey, my upstairs neighbor, walked around the community arguing with himself, mostly about government conspiracies? Would they know he was harmless? Would they know his path, so they didn't pass him when giving a tour to a prospective resident?

No, I guess they wouldn't.

I unlocked the lobby door, and my thoughts turned to Violet's daughter. Would she fly out to help with the investigation? If she...

What in the world?

Tires screeched against asphalt, and the familiar scent of burnt rubber filled the air. The gate rolled opened, and a brown Buick peeled out. As it passed, I checked the driver's side. The same man from earlier, the one with the wrinkled suit, sat at the wheel with a cigarette hanging from his mouth. I used my hand as a visor, hoping to make out his license plate, but he was gone too fast.

CHAPTER EIGHT

———

—I'm a seven.

The phone rang in my ear while I paced along the side of the pool, donning the new swimsuit I'd recently bought online. A black one-piece that was 10% nylon, 90% Spanx, and I 100% couldn't breathe in it. Hampton didn't answer, and I was connected to his voicemail. Frustrated, I hung up and called again. The pavement burnt the bottom of my feet, and I dipped them into the water and kept pacing.

This time, he answered. "Detective Hampton."

"I have a problem."

"Hi, Cambria."

"A guy is snooping around my community, and I just caught him racing out of the parking lot. I think he's connected to Violet's disappearance somehow." I plugged one ear to better hear over Lilly and Kevin, who were playing a game of Marco Polo in the shallow end. "Help me out."

"Did you get a license plate?"

"No, because he was *speeding*. Stay with me, Hampton." I stopped and dipped my feet into the pool then resumed pacing. "He's an older guy, gray hair, drives a brown Buick."

"That narrows it down."

"This is no time to get a sense of humor!" No time at all. "Right after Violet disappears, this strange man shows up and is lurking around the apartments. He's looking for residents but doesn't have their apartment numbers. Coincidence? Methinks not."

"You're right. I'm sorry."

"No time for apologies. Did you get my text?"

"The picture of the dirty baseboard?"

"Yes! What was found in the stairwell? Why isn't there a sign on Violet's door? Do you have any leads? Have you talked to the owners?" I stopped to dip my feet. "Did you check the elevator?"

"I promise we're working on it. But have you entertained the idea that Violet left on her own free will?" he asked.

No, I hadn't.

Huh?

But if she were determined to stay, enough to hire a lawyer when the Dashwoods tried to fire her, then why would she take off without her wallet or phone?

"Nope," I decided. "There's no way. This has foul play written all over it. What's going on with my sketch? Do you know what I had to go through in order to get that done? Have you ever dealt with a tired three-year-old? Stormy hadn't even seen it yet."

"Tell me you didn't take a picture of it with your phone and show her?"

"Um…" I stopped pacing. That was exactly what happened. "What if I did?"

"When I show someone a sketch, I want to be able to read their initial reaction. Now I don't have that."

Good point.

An excellent point.

Note to self: stupid move, Cambria.

I wasn't sure what to say, so I said nothing.

Which answered his question.

"Cambria."

"Yes."

"Please let me handle this investigation."

"For what it's worth, I don't think Stormy had anything to do with Violet's disappearance. She seems harmless and somewhat incompetent. But in a charming way."

"Incompetently charming. Got it. I'll make a note of that. As for your guy, next time you see him, take a picture or get his license plate. I'll send out a description. We have Cedar Creek under surveillance, so I wouldn't worry. OK."

"Good. Also, I have another problem. One of my residents fell off the roof yesterday, and I think the police thought he...hello?"

I looked down at my phone.

Hampton hung up on me.

Geez. I was losing even more confidence in his ability to find Violet. I tossed my phone onto a chair and took a seat on the second step in the pool. The water came up my waist, and I dropped my elbows on my knees.

Kevin swam over. "What's up your a—"

"Bleep!" I jerked my head toward Lilly, who stood at the side of the pool with her pink floaties on, summoning the courage required to jump in.

"Fine. What's up your bleep?"

"Violet."

"That sounds uncomfortable."

"Not funny."

OK, it was a little funny.

I wrapped my arms around my legs and pulled my knees to my chest. *I should have shaved last night.* "A suspicious guy is lurking around here. Chase is on a special assignment, and I'm worried he'll die. I'm concerned about Larry. We're closing in on twenty-four hours since Violet disappeared. My mom said I have a thankless job and I'd be a more well-rounded person if I had siblings, and now I think I should have another baby so Lilly doesn't grow up to be just like me."

Kevin took a seat. "Who needs a sibling? I'm an only child and turned out fine."

"You just got out of prison."

"*Because* I had a drug problem, not because I killed anyone."

"You were also arrested for public nudity."

"You make a good point. Have another baby."

"It's not that simple."

"Sure it is. Have another baby with Chase or Tom." He shook his head. "How you have *those* two men to choose from is beyond me."

"I don't have two to choose from, and, what's that supposed to mean?"

We stopped to watch Lilly jump from the side of the pool. We clapped. We cheered. We gave her a thumbs-up. Then went back to chatting. "They're both tens," Kevin said. "I'd go with Tom. I like brunettes. Plus you don't want too many baby daddies."

True.

I had serious doubt Chase would be OK with Tom and I procreating again. I had serious doubt Chase would be OK procreating with me right now. We'd never talked about kids. Though he did adore Lilly. We'd never talked about marriage. Though he did treat me well.

And I was pretty sure I loved him.

So there was that.

"What do you think I am?" I asked Kevin. "On the hotness scale?"

Kevin studied me under intense scrutiny. "I'd say you're a seven."

I sat up a little straighter. "That's not bad." Not bad at all.

"If you did something with your hair, you'd be an eight."

"I'll take that into consideration."

"A tattoo might be hot."

I bit the corner of my lip. "I have one."

Kevin leaned back and stared as if he were seeing me for the first time. "Don't tell me you have a tramp stamp."

I nodded. "It's a dolphin." When Amy and I first moved to Los Angeles, we'd decided to get matching tattoos to commemorate our voyage. Except she chickened out after she saw how painful mine was. Now I was stuck with Flipper forever.

"I don't believe you."

I checked to be sure no residents were watching. Not that I was ashamed of my dolphin (actually, I hated it), but it would take some creative maneuvering to show Kevin in my restrictive swimsuit. I lifted one butt cheek out of the water and shifted the bottom of my suit, giving myself a painful wedgie. I had no idea how Hampton walked around like that all day. "Do you see it?"

"No. Hold still." Kevin pulled the back of my suit away from my skin and peered down. "I can almost see it. Sit up a little more."

"What are you two doing?"

Kevin and I looked up. Tom stood over us with his mirror lens aviators on, dressed in slacks and brown loafers. Kevin let go of my bathing suit, and it snapped against my skin. *Ouch.*

"I was checking out her tat," Kevin said.

"Aw, yes, the dolphin." Tom removed his sunglasses and tucked them into the top of his shirt. His right eye encircled in hues of blue and yellow. "I remember it well."

I felt my cheeks flush and turned away. Tom and I were so drunk the night we made Lilly, I was surprised he remembered anything.

"Daddy!" Lilly kicked to the steps and climbed out of the pool. "Daddy, watch what I can do." She plugged her nose and jumped in.

We clapped. We cheered. We gave her a thumbs-up. Then went back to chatting.

"Sorry, I didn't realize it was so late." I stepped out of the pool. "I'll get her stuff ready."

"I like your bathing suit." Tom followed me to the chair. I could feel his gaze on my backside.

"Oh, this old thing?" I grabbed a towel and wrapped it around my waist.

"I have these for you." Tom pulled two coupons for a car wash from his shirt pocket. "Tell them I sent you, and ask for Carlos."

"I think my car is beyond a detailing, but thank you." Tom's clients typically paid for his lawyering abilities by way of bartering. He had a lifetime supply of burritos from Casa Grande Cafe but barely enough in his checking account to cover child support. It was hard to fault him for following his moral compass.

"Did you talk to the boyfriend about New York yet?"

It *was,* however, easy to fault him for trying to insert himself into my relationship with Chase. "No, because he's in Texas."

"What's he doing in Texas?"

"Working, if you must know."

"I thought he was a detective for the LAPD."

"He is."

"Why would the LAPD send a detective to Texas?"

I wavered. But if Chase said he had work to do in Texas, then he had work to do in Texas. He too had a moral compass. "Tom"—I drew out his name—"the only reason you want to come with me to New York is because you don't want me to go with anyone else. If I were going by myself, you'd have no problem."

"I didn't say I had a problem. I just asked if you talked to Chase yet."

Oh.

"But if you want me to go, I'm happy to do so." He flashed his signature side smirk, and I took note of the lipstick stain on his collar. *Ugh.* I threw my hands up in the air and let out a grunt. The man was infuriating.

Tom had four older brothers. *Four!* And he was just as screwed up as the rest of us only children.

Which oddly made me feel better.

I swiped Lilly's towel from the chair. "Time to go, sweetie."

"Me want to stay here with you," she said. Which also made me feel better.

"You're going to come with me, kiddo," Tom said. "We'll get dinner and play at McDonald's. Sound good?"

"Yay!" Lilly kicked as hard as she could to the stairs and climbed out of the pool.

There was no competing with McDonald's PlayPlace, unfortunately. "You'll be sure she wears socks in the structure and sanitize her hands when she gets out?"

"Do I look like an amateur parent?"

"The plastic tunnels on those play structures have three hundred eighty times more bacteria in them than a household toilet," I said. "I read it on WebMD."

"Thanks for ruining play structures." Tom wrapped the towel around Lilly and scooped her up in his arms. "Did they find the apartment manager next door?"

I took Lilly's sandals out of my bag and put them on her feet. "Not yet. It's been almost a full twenty-four hours."

"Are you sure you're safe here?"

Noooo. "Yes."

"Can we talk more about New York?"

"No." My cell buzzed from the chair. A number I didn't recognize flashed across the screen. "Hold on. Let me answer this." I sandwiched the phone between my shoulder and ear and continued to gather Lilly's stuff. "This is Cambria."

"It's Stormy. Remember when you said to call you if I needed help managing this place?"

I didn't remember saying those exact words but, "Sure. What's going on?"

CHAPTER NINE

———

—Pinterest makes me feel productive.

"What did you do?" I pulled my sweatshirt over my head and took a seat at Stormy's desk.

"I don't know!" Stormy fanned her red sweaty face. "I looked up YouTube like you said, and this message came up."

Across the screen it said *Your Computer Has Been Locked* in big, bold, blocky print with the FBI symbol on the side. A phone number was displayed at the bottom of the message, warning a fine of two hundred dollars had to be paid within twenty-four hours or the computer would be wiped clean. It looked about as legit as the daily emails I got from the California Lotto office located in Kenya wanting to speak to me about my unclaimed winnings.

"I've heard about this. It's a virus. Do you have malware protection on this computer?"

Stormy stared at me.

"This is a work computer," I said. "I'm sure you do."

"I called the number at the bottom of the screen and gave them my credit card information, and it didn't work," she said.

Oh geez. "What other information did you give them?"

"My social security number, phone number, address, date of birth, and my mother's maiden name."

That's not good. "If I were you, I'd call your credit card company and fight the charges and close that card. In the meantime, I think we can turn this off." I searched under the desk for the modem and held the power button until the screen turned black and the Windows logo returned.

"Wow," Stormy said as if I'd just performed a magic trick.

I checked my watch. "Why are you here so late?"

"I typically work until seven."

That's a bummer. "Give it a minute to power up, and then you should be able to continue."

"That's the problem. I don't know *how* to continue." She sat on the desk and used a brochure advertising their luxury three-bedroom apartment homes as a fan. "I just spoke to the owners, and I panicked. That's when I tried to search the internet to see how to do my job like you said."

"Why were you panicking?"

"They need a vacancy report by Thursday."

"They know about Violet, right? I'm sure they'll give you leeway, considering."

"They know about Violet. Detective Hampton called them. They said they were sorry but they're in the process of doing an audit and really need the information."

Audit?

This felt like an important piece of information. I remembered what Patrick said about Dick Dashwood asking for tax and finance guy recommendations.

"Then they said they were confident the building was in good hands," Stormy said. "Problem is, I don't know the first thing about managing this place."

"What exactly *do* you do normally?"

"I send out the monthly newsletter and organize community events. Last month we had a movie night. Before that, we had a carnival. I change the air fresheners every month. I take care of the kids' corner, and I stock the Wow Fridge."

"What's a Wow Fridge?"

A moment later I stood in front of a stainless-steel refrigerator with my mouth wide open. "Wow," was all I could say. Inside were rows of yellow Gatorade, water bottles with the Cedar Creek logo wrapped around them, sparkling lemonade, packages of fish crackers, candy, chips, and soda.

"Every month I choose a theme," Stormy said proudly. "Since it's summer, I went with yellow."

"Why do you put pantry items in the fridge?"

"That's what makes it *wow*, and to fill it up. There's only so much cold yellow stuff you can buy."

"And this is for residents?"

"It's for everyone. Look." She opened the freezer, and inside were popsicles, ice cream, Drumsticks, and fudge sundaes.

I'm in heaven.

"Grab whatever you want."

Don't mind if I do.

I helped myself to a bag of Lays and an ice cream sandwich. Which shouldn't melt for awhile since it was still roughly five degrees inside the office.

Back behind Stormy's desk, I unwrapped my sandwich. The computer was on with no fake FBI warnings. "I can help you with your report. We use the same software program you do."

"How do you know what program we use?"

"See that symbol down there?" I pointed to the big *P* on her desktop. "That stands for Panda. It's a management software." I pulled up her vacancy report. "There it is...oh wait."

"What's wrong?"

"This can't be accurate, because it lists Apartment 105 as vacant, and that's where Dolores lives. It must not be updated. Although..." I scrolled to the bottom of the page. The report showed apartments 306, 402, 610, 509, 508, 404, 903, 314, 407, 612, and 101 also as vacant, equaling twelve in total. "Violet said you had twelve vacancies when I spoke to her Monday." I clicked on Apartment 105, which, according to the report, showed the last resident had moved out in January. Six months for a vacancy is a long time. If Dolores had just received a rental increase, then she must have lived there at least a year. I searched for Dolores Rocklynn.

Zero results found.

"That's odd," I said more to myself than Stormy. I deleted Dolores Rocklynn and spelled it three different ways. All came up with zero results. I ripped a Post-it from the stack and wrote down *Dolores Rocklynn Apartment 105.* "Check through your hard copy files to see if you can find her."

"We don't have hard copy files."

"Why not?"

"Violet said it wasn't necessary."

Oh. Um... I blew out a breath. "Ask Antonio for help with vacancies. He turns them, so he should know."

"What do you mean *turn*?"

Geez. Stormy really didn't know anything about the business. "Turn" is basic industry lingo. "Prepare for rental after a move-out," I said.

"Oh! I think we have an outside vendor turn the units, and Violet supervises."

"Why wouldn't your maintenance supervisor *supervise*?"

"He fills maintenance requests."

It sure felt like Violet wasn't utilizing her staff. Granted, I'd never had an assistant manager, so who was I to judge. Also, I might not trust Stormy with our management software either. "Antonio should know what's vacant and what's not if he's doing maintenance requests." I stuck the note to her monitor. "And please keep an eye out for a guy with gray hair driving a brown Buick, please. I caught him lurking around my community. He may know something about Violet."

"Aye-aye, Captain." She stood at attention and gave me a salute.

A ping of panic stabbed my heart.

I didn't want to be the captain of this ship.

* * *

I was home by eight. All was quiet, but I locked the doors and windows, set the alarms, and closed the blinds. I forwent the shower and decided on dessert instead. I stripped down to my underwear and a tank top and sat on my bed with my laptop open, the fan blasting, and a bowl of double fudge melting at my side. I searched preschools in the area that offered full-day options. Turned out I needed a second and third job to pay for them.

Who knew learning the ABCs would cost my retirement fund.

OK, that was a lie.

I didn't have a retirement fund.

But still!

I switched over to Pinterest and searched for three-year-old quiet time activities. Somehow, pinning made me feel like a better parent.

My phone rang. I crossed my fingers, hoping it wasn't the emergency line.

It was Chase requesting to FaceTime.

Crap!

I licked the ice cream from my fingertips and scooted to the bathroom to check my appearance in the mirror. I had chocolate on my nose, and Einstein could be seen from space. I tamed the mane, wiped my face, held the phone up high, and accepted his request. His cute face filled the screen, and I ached to see him in real life. "Hey you," I greeted with, what I hoped was, a seductive smolder.

"There you are. I tried calling you earlier."

"I was next door helping out the assistant manager."

Chase swung an arm behind his head. He was lying down in a hotel bed. I could tell by the bleached white sheets and matching pillowcase.

"How'd the meeting with the sketch artist go?"

"Good." I lay down on my bed and held the phone up. "I think Hampton is annoyed by me."

"I *know* he is," he said with a wink.

Well then. "It's just that I can't stop thinking about Violet. It's been over twenty-four hours, and I don't think Hampton is following any of our leads."

"Our?"

"I meant it royally." Obviously.

"*Royally* would mean *me*."

"Exactly."

Chase relented. "What leads do you have?"

I sucked in a breath and told him about Dolores, and the owners, and the man in a Buick, and, of course, there was Stairwell Man.

"Cambria, I know you're concerned, but Hampton could have ruled out those suspects already, or he's currently investigating them," Chase said. "You realize he doesn't need to discuss the details of the case with you, right?"

He made a point.

"I just keep going over the timing of everything," I said. "I received the first call about her bathtub at 8:12 PM. Dolores said the water had been leaking from the ceiling for ten minutes. Then at 9:50 PM I received a second call. This time the water and the ceiling were coming down, but when I showed up, she wouldn't let me in. Clearly something had happened to Violet before the first call. The window was open in the closet, but it would be really hard to drag a body out of that window and go unnoticed. My guess would be someone entered through the window and went down the stairs, except the lobby would be too obvious. They must have gone through the outside parking lot. Which backs up to our place..." A horrendous thought trotted into my head. I tried to shake it away, but it trotted right back.

"What are you thinking?" Chase asked.

"I'm going to show you the ceiling fan for a minute." I put my phone down and swung my legs over the side of the bed.

—*Larry was on the roof right after I received the first call from Dolores.*

—*Kevin did say locking yourself out on the patio is impossible.*

—*Larry was not permitted to have unauthorized visitors at the hospital.*

—*Hampton had not shown Stormy the sketch yet. Wouldn't that be a priority one? Unless he already had a suspect in custody.*

—*Could Larry have been involved, run from Cedar Creek, climbed the fence into Julia's patio, desperate to escape and hide, not been able to get in, and decided to use the roof to get to his apartment instead?*

I slid open my patio door, flipped the lock, stepped outside, and slid the door shut. Stupid move, I suddenly realized. My phone was on my bed. I was outside wearing nothing but underwear and a tank.

Smooth, Cambria. Real smooth.

I imagined having to climb the fence, run across the front lawn, wait for a car to leave so I could enter the property through the gate—which could be awhile since most residents were home for the night—sneak to the back, and ask Mr. Nguyen to let me in. All the while running around in my underwear. Not good.

Lucky for me, it turned out not to be a problem. The door wouldn't close all the way with the lock on.

But there's no way Larry could have...right?

CHAPTER TEN

—Just when you link you've seen it all, a bird shows up in lingerie.

...Nah.

Larry wouldn't hurt a fly. Two weeks earlier, the pest control company tried to remove a beehive from under the back stairwell, and Larry staged a protest, positioning himself in front of the hive and refusing to move. While I appreciated his stance, I had five other residents cowering in their apartments, alleging to be deathly allergic and/or deathly afraid of bees, threatening to sue and/or call Fair Housing if the hive was not removed.

Multiple bee stings later and Larry had agreed to end his protest if I promised to have the hive relocated. This did not sound like a man capable of hurting anyone. Yet my patio didn't lock from the outside, and he was on the roof right around the time Violet went missing. A coincidence I couldn't overlook.

I told Chase I would call him tomorrow and slipped on a pair of shorts. The weather had cooled, and I cut through the community with my arms wrapped around my chest, wishing I'd put on a bra. It was late and dark, and the windows around the property were lit by the glow of a television or a single reading light. I could hear the hum of cars speeding down Sepulveda and indistinct chatter from those walking down the street. Dogs erupted into a chorus of panicking barks as I walked by. Pretty sure they were trained to alert the owners of my presence. I rarely heard them bark otherwise.

Larry lived in the third courtyard, near the breezeway he'd climbed across. His lights were off, but I knocked anyway.

Silvia Kravitz opened her door instead. *Great.* Harold, her parrot, was perched on her shoulder.

Does that bird ever see his cage?

The two had on matching blue nighties. I had no idea they made lingerie for parrots.

"Larry isn't home." Silvia placed a hand on her hip, and Harold turned his backside to me. "They're releasing him tomorrow."

"When did you talk to him?"

"I went to see him this morning,"

"You were able to?" I squeaked in surprised.

"What are you going to do about the roof? It's clearly unsafe."

"Of course it is. It's a roof."

"Then you should have a caution sign warning people not to go up there."

Random fact: when you're a property manager, you hear something new and stupid every day.

More importantly, how had Silvia been authorized and I wasn't?

"I can't put a label on everything," I said. "At some point common sense needs to be used."

If Silvia could move her face, I think she'd be scowling. "I don't want to see something like this happen again. The poor sweet man has two broken legs and three cracked ribs."

Poor sweet man?

I tried not to laugh.

Not because Larry was hurt, of course. But because a month earlier Silvia had called Larry an inconsiderate buffoon because she could hear him peeing though the "paper thin" walls at six AM.

"I'll look into adding this information to our House Rules," I said to appease her. I'd learned any battle with Silvia was a losing one.

I also learned that no one actually read the House Rules, so she'd never know.

"Good. It's about time you make the safety of the residents here a priority. Now, good night."

I waited until she closed the door before I flipped her off.

Then I felt bad.

Then I got over it.

I jolted down the stairs. When I hit the ground, my knee buckled, and I crashed onto the cement.

Karma for flipping off a resident.

Or just a bum knee.

Either way, it took every ounce of willpower I had not to scream. Instead, I hobbled around in agony until I could bend my leg again.

Note to self: go see a knee doctor, ASAP.

Once I regained my composure, I stood directly below Larry's patio, rubbing my sore kneecap. Legally, I couldn't enter his apartment to check the lock on the sliding door. I could, however, climb up and look at his lock from outside.

I returned with the folding stepladder from the maintenance garage. It looked as old as the building, and not exactly stable, but it was all we had. I spread it apart and positioned it under Larry's patio. One step up and the metal creaked as if it were being tortured. Another step up and my knee clicked. Another step up and I could already see my obituary.

Cambria Jane Clyne (pronounced Came-bree-a) plummeted to her death late Tuesday evening while snooping. She is survived by her daughter, Lilly Clyne Dryer, her loving parents (plus that woman her dad married), a boyfriend, and baby daddy, both who are tens on the hotness scale even if she was a seven. Cambria's hobbies included eating ice cream and watching crime shows. She won her third grade spelling bee and managed no noteworthy achievements since.

Nope.

Not how I wanted to die.

I needed backup.

* * *

"You want me to climb up that thing?" Kevin was in his boxer shorts and mismatched socks, with his hands on his head and apprehension on his face. "It's like a hundred years old."

"No it's not. I'll hold it steady for you. It's not that far up."

"Then why don't you do it and I'll hold it?"

"I don't trust my knee. Come on." I held the ladder with both hands. "Up you go."

Kevin climbed the first three steps. "What am I doing once I'm up there?"

"Take a picture of the lock on Larry's patio door."

He let out a laugh. "I told you it's not possible to lock yourself out."

"Fine. You were right, and I was wrong. Maybe. We don't know. He could have a different lock than I do. Just take the picture and hurry up before anyone sees us."

Kevin climbed the rest of the way. The ladder began to teeter, and I used all my weight to keep it from tipping. He pulled his phone from between the elastic of his boxers and his skin and snapped a picture. "The things I do for you," he grumbled.

"I fed your snake while you were locked up. The least you can do is take a picture for me."

"Whatever. OK, I took it. Now what?"

"Is there a lock on the outside?"

"Mmmhmmm. It's the same one I have on mine… Now that I think about it, I've locked myself out on my patio before."

"I'm going to kill you!" I moved, and the ladder teetered on two feet. Kevin grabbed hold of the railing.

"Are you crazy, woman?"

"Sorry, I wasn't *actually* trying to kill you." I sat on the opposite side of the ladder and spread my feet apart, creating a secure anchor. "I've got it. Go ahead."

"Are you sure?"

"Yes, I'm sure. Trust me."

"I did trust you until you threatened to kill me."

"It was a figure of speech. Go ahead."

He descended, carefully.

I felt better knowing Larry's story checked out. Besides, what would have been his motivation to hurt Violet? I had serious doubts the two knew each other. Which still begged the question: what *did* happen to Violet?

Also, why was Silvia authorized to see him and I wasn't? Silvia constantly berated the man for every little thing he did, while I patiently listened to him talk about all his physical ailments (and he had a lot of them). Hell, last week I weighed in on the suspicious boil on his back. He showed me a picture, and even though that image haunted my dreams for the next three days, I still looked up a dermatologist for him.

Mom was right—my job was thankless.

I was deep in thought and not paying attention, and without warning, Kevin jumped down the remaining two steps, and the ladder collapsed on top of me.

In lieu of flowers, the family has asked you donate to Lilly's preschool fund.

CHAPTER ELEVEN

———

—Property management is hard on the body.

The next morning I felt like I'd been run over by a semi. Or…errrr…a ladder.

I reached for the water on my nightstand, but it was too far, and I was too tired, and life suddenly felt too hard. I clambered out of bed and did my pee-weigh-myself-declare-diet-starts-tomorrow routine. I even managed to get dressed in jeans, a navy V-neck, and white Converse. I did not, however, take a shower and shave my legs.

Note to self: do both before Chase gets home.
Sub-note: or at least one of the two.

Before the clock struck nine, I sent a good morning text to Chase, unlocked the lobby doors—allowing for pass-through traffic—grabbed the cordless phone from my desk, and sat on the couch with the remote control clutched in my hand. The stupid thing was broken, and it took a few hard shakes to get it to work. I settled on a rerun of my favorite crime drama, *If Only*, and curled around a throw pillow. The beauty of working from home is, you can watch TV when it's slow or, in this case, when you felt as if your body had aged fifty years overnight.

The only problem was, while being an on-site apartment manager allowed for downtime, being a mother did not. Tom's tall shadow drifted across the wall. I *one…two…three…*heaved my body off the couch and opened the door. Lilly had on pink overalls and a white shirt with roses on it. Toothpaste crusted the outer corners of her mouth and her hair… Oh, her hair…it looked as if she'd rubbed a balloon across her head.

Poor thing inherited her own Einstein.

Tom removed his sunglasses and flashed his signature side smirk. "Good morning, Cam."

"Morning. Give me." I pointed to Lilly's go-between bag, and he draped it over my arm.

"I need to talk to you. Can we meet up tonight?"

"No."

"Why not?"

"I'm not doing this with you anymore. We co-parent. That's it."

"What if the reason I want to meet up is to talk about our kid?"

"Is it about our kid?"

"No."

For the love!

"Tom, I'm done riding this roller coaster with you. Tonight, my *boyfriend* is calling, and tomorrow he comes home. Would you like to take Lilly so he and I could spend time together?"

Tom was shaking his head before I even finished speaking.

"I guess it's settled then. I'll see you Friday. Have a good day in court." I swung the door shut with my hip and padded back to the couch, feeling quite proud of myself. There was a time, not too long ago, when I'd get hung up on every word out of Tom's mouth, grasping for a sign he cared about me more than just a friend. There were far too many instances where he wanted to "talk" and I'd get my hopes up, only to have them crushed. I'd wasted too many tears over that man.

Now, I was able to stick to my convictions.

Perhaps I *did* have superhuman powers after all.

Lilly parked herself on the couch, kicked off her shoes, grabbed the remote control, and gave it a few hard shakes.

"Not today." I pried the remote from her grasp. "No television. We're limiting screen time."

She looked at me as if I'd lost my mind, but according to the twenty new parenting pins I'd read on Pinterest, Lilly should have less screen time and more problem-solving activities.

I retrieved a box of Q-tips from my bathroom, a colander from the kitchen, and sat on the floor.

"Are we making noodles?" Lilly asked.

"No. We're working on fine motor skills. Watch." I shoved a Q-tip into a hole of the colander. Then another, and another. It was therapeutic, and before I knew it, I'd gone through an entire package of Q-tips while Lilly played on my phone.

"Someone is calling you." Lilly turned to show me. A familiar number flashed across the screen.

* * *

"How'd you do this?" All the icons on Stormy's computer screen were gone.

"I was trying to arrange the little pictures, and then, *poof!* They weren't there anymore." Stormy was on the other side of her desk, hyperventilating. "I don't think I'm cut out for this job. I like stocking the Wow Fridge and organizing community events. It doesn't require a computer."

"I'm sure it will be fine," I said, which, of course, was a lie. Even the trash icon was gone, and I had no idea how to help her. "Let's restart the computer. I'll check YouTube when I get back to my office and let you know what I find." I got up and pushed her chair back under the desk. "Let's go, sweetie," I called to Lilly, who was at the Kid's Corner.

"That detective came in this morning and showed me the sketch," Stormy said.

I sat back down. "Did it look familiar this time?"

She shook her head. "There are so many people coming and going from here, though."

"Did he say anything more about Violet? Do you know if they have any leads?"

"I don't know. He asked if I knew of a reason why she would *want* to disappear."

"Could you think of one?"

She shook her head no.

"Did he ask about the owners or visit Dolores's apartment?"

She shook her head no.

Ugh.

I rubbed my throat. The situation gave me indigestion, and we were closing in on the forty-eight-hour mark. "It's the unknown that's so unnerving," I said. "Where did she go? Is she alive? Who took her? Did she...struggle?"

Stormy looked over at Violet's empty desk. "Agreed."

We sat in silence for a moment, reflecting, when I remembered, "Did you get the list of vacancies from Antonio?"

"I did," she almost sang, and handed me a Post-it with three apartments written in her familiar chicken scratch.

Three?

"When I spoke to Violet on Monday, she said you have twelve vacancies. Maybe these are the ones that are rent ready, but...if you hire out, then you should have more than three rent ready. Unless you stagger them...which wouldn't make sense because you need to reconcile the deposit within 21 days..." I was baffled by the discrepancy in vacancies. Apartment managers don't over exaggerate their vacancies. If anything, they lied and say they had less. It didn't make any sense.

"What should I do?" Stormy batted her heavily make-upped eyes.

Note to self: This is not your job, Cambria. This is not your job. This is not your job. This is not your job. Get up and walk away.

I stood before I talked myself out of it. If I wasn't careful, I'd end up managing Cedar Creek as well. "This is a good start. If someone wants to see a vacant unit, you can show them one of the three on the list."

"What do I do after I show them the apartment?"

It took every ounce of self-control I had not to gawk at her. "You give them an application if they're interested. I'm sure you have pamphlets with the community amenities outlined and your business card."

She wrung her hands.

"Do you know where the applications are?" I asked, already knowing the answer.

"I know they're on a tablet."

"Good. Where's the tablet?" I asked.

She wrung her hands.

Note to self: This is not your job, Cambria. This is not your job, Cambria. This is not your job…

Who was I kidding?

I couldn't *not* help her. I'm a fixer. It's what I do. Apparently, if I had siblings I wouldn't be so inclined.

"I'm sure the tablet is somewhere around here," I said. "I'll print you out a few applications from the Fair Housing website if you can't find it."

I could almost see the little light bulb in Stormy's head turn on. "I saw a tablet in the storage room." She shuffled down a hallway outside the office, and I followed. Why? I don't know.

The hall had a beautiful distressed cream-colored runner down the middle with little blue and pale yellow flowers on it. Two dark blue cabinets adorned each side, with a gold-rimmed mirror above.

Three doors lined the hall. Two had the all-gender restroom sign hung in the middle, one was closed, and a single door ended the hallway and was labeled *Maintenance*.

Antonio had his own office? Must be nice. Mr. Nguyen had the maintenance garage only. It was dark and musty and known to harbor a brown widow or two.

Stormy opened the unlabeled door and flipped on the light. Wire shelving and filing cabinets along with discarded office furnishing filled the space.

I couldn't imagine why they would keep the tablets in the file room. You'd want something like that easily accessible. "Are you sure it's not in the office?"

Stormy slid a box of file folders over. "If it is, I haven't seen it."

"How about you look in here, and I'll check the office."

I went back down the hall. If Violet handled all the leases, my best guess was the tablet was in her desk. I took a seat in her chair, and it slowly sunk until the edge of the desk lined up with my boobs, making a whizzing sound on my way down, like air being let out of a tire.

Well that was fun.

Whatever.

Violet ate green stuff.

I didn't.

It felt intrusive going through Violet's personal space, and I was careful not to disturb anything as I looked around.

Much like her apartment, Violet's desk was well organized. No stray staples or even a paper clip could be found out of place. Inspirational quotes were written in lovely script on sticky notes and stuck around the perimeter of her monitor.

If you don't sacrifice for what you want, you'll never get it!

Give yourself permission to live a big life.

The ladder to success is made from the shoulders of those who are too weak to go for it.

Don't be afraid to do whatever it takes. You only have one life.

Well...OK. They weren't so much inspirational as they were...*motivational?*

Property management is a crazy business. If stepping on people's shoulders helped Violet cope, then it wasn't my place to judge.

On the bottom of the screen were two Post-its with tally marks. Cedar Creek had 255 units, yet there were well over a thousand tally marks. I pulled open the bottom drawer and found Violet's other coping mechanism—an opened box of Twinkies. Beneath was a copy of *Daily C-Leb Magazine*. It was an older issue, released the day the cast of *Celebrity Tango* was announced. Amy was front and center, wearing a sequined bra and shimmery pants that looked as if they were made of discarded disco ball parts.

I flipped through the magazine. The page with Raven's bio was dog-eared and *-110* was written in the same swirly handwriting in the margin.

Interesting...

My phone buzzed in my back pocket. I thunked the heel of my hand against my forehead when I saw it was the emergency line.

"Hello," I said once connected.

"Apartment Manager, it is Silvia Kravitz. There is a man snooping around the third courtyard. It's quite unnerving." I heard the rattle of the vertical blinds swinging on the hooks, and

I pictured Silvia peeping out her window. "He is peeking into enclosed patios. I saw him doing this yesterday evening, too!"

I put the magazine back and closed the drawer. "Can you take a picture of him for me?"

"*No*, because I'm on my phone." Now I imagined her rolling her eyes.

"You can still take a picture when you're on your phone... Never mind. I'll be right there." I hung up and put Violet's desk back as I found it.

Stormy appeared with a tablet in hand. "Where are you going?" she asked in a panic.

"I have to work."

"But...but...but..."

"Lilly! We need to leave right now." I held out my hand.

Lilly dropped the crayons and hurried, holding the picture she was working on. I pushed open the whimsical doors. Stormy was at my side. "You'll be fine," I assured her.

"But—"

"I'm sorry. I need to go." With Lilly on my hip, I ran as fast I could.

"I don't like Stormy," Lilly said as I ran.

"That's not a nice thing to say." I unlocked the pedestrian gate, ran through the carports, under the archway, through the first courtyard, and past the pool.

"She looks like Ursula," Lilly said, holding on tight to my neck.

I laughed. Mostly because it was true. Stormy did resemble the sea witch from *The Little Mermaid*—minus the tentacles.

"Please don't ever say that to her," I huffed out, still frantically searching through the community. I did four loops around the property, peeking into carports, patios, and checking the storage closet. I called Daniella again, but she didn't answer.

The man was nowhere to be found.

CHAPTER TWELVE

———

—Resourcefulness is key to survival.
So is caffeine.

"Why'd I bring my sketch pad?" Kevin stepped inside and closed the door. He had on tan khaki shorts with a hole in the back pocket. I could smell the Pantene and Dove on his skin as he brushed past me on the way to the kitchen.

"I need you to draw a picture of the man I saw snooping around here. He came back today and, according to Silvia, he was here last night." I took a seat at the table and pulled out a chair for Kevin.

"Where's the kid?" He grabbed two spoons from the top drawer and a pint of Ben & Jerry's Chunky Monkey ice cream from the freezer. A fitting choice of flavor given my circus currently had too many monkeys.

"She's in bed."

Kevin gazed out the window. "It's still light out."

"According to WebMD, three-year-olds need eleven hours of sleep a day and, in order to achieve this, she needs to be in bed by seven. And—"

"Yeah, I don't need a novel." He took a seat and handed me a spoon.

"Thanks." I took a bite of ice cream then crossed my legs and got comfortable. "Let's do this." I closed my eyes and pulled up an image of the man from the breezeway. "He's likely in his sixties, with a long forehead and a—"

Kevin sharpened his pencil, and my eyes popped open. "Aren't you supposed to do that *before* you start?"

"I didn't say I was ready—you just began jabbering away." He blew off the excess shavings from the tip and sat straight-backed with his pad in front of him. "I'm ready."

"Finally!" I was anxious to get this done. Violet had been missing almost forty-eight hours, and if this man had anything to do with her disappearance, then he had to be found, ASAP. I closed my eyes and brought the image back up. I tried to remember the questions Calvin asked and answered them out loud. *Wispy hair...sunken cheeks...vertical wrinkles down his face...*

When finished, Kevin studied the picture with a curious tilt of his head. "Do you recognize him?" I asked.

"I do." He turned the pad around. "Looks like Clint Eastwood."

I squinted. "You're right. Why do all my sketches look like celebrities?"

He shrugged. "Cause we're in LA?"

I snapped a picture of the sketch with my phone and sent it to Hampton.

My phone rang. "What am I looking at now?" he asked.

In the background, I could hear indecipherable talking and the clinking of silverware on plates. The thought of Hampton dining out with his pants hiked high and his toupee on crooked, enjoying himself while Violet lay in a ditch somewhere, or tied up in a barnyard, or shoved in the back of a taxi...

I really do need to lay off the crime shows.

Anyway. The thought of Hampton leisurely enjoying a night off brought my blood to a boil. "Shouldn't you be working?"

"I *am* working, Cambria. I stepped away from an interview to call you."

Oh.

Oops.

I cleared my throat. "I sent you a sketch of the man I found snooping around in my community. The one who drives a brown Buick. Does he look familiar?"

"Looks like Clint Eastwood?"

"He does look similar, yes," I said.

"So I'm looking for Danny Tanner and Dirty Harry."

"Who's Dirty Harry?" I asked.

"You've never seen *Dirty Harry*?" Both Kevin and Hampton said simultaneously, Kevin gaping at me.

"No," I said, feeling a bit defensive. *Dirty Harry* sounded more like a drink than a movie.

"It's about a cop who attempts to track down a psychopathic rooftop killer before a kidnapped girl dies," Kevin explained. "Starring Clint Eastwood."

Sounded good, but we weren't there to talk movies. We had to find Violet. I checked the time on the clock above the stove. It had officially been forty-eight hours.

"It's a good sketch," Hampton said. "I'll have my guys look into it and see what we come up with."

"Are you any closer to finding her?" I pushed the ice cream away. No longer hungry. You know a situation is dire when frozen slow-churned sugar and cream with bits of fudge won't help.

"We're working on it," he said, but he didn't sound confident. He didn't sound confident at all.

I hugged my legs to my chest. "How did her daughter take the news? Is she coming out?"

"I...can't talk right now. I'll see if we can find a match for Dirty Harry in the system. OK."

"Can you at least...hello?" I looked down at my phone. Hampton hung up on me. Again!

Ugh.

With nothing more to do, Kevin and I retreated to the couch with Ben & Jerry in tow. I switched all the fans to high speed, and Kevin turned on the rerun of *If Only*, the one I'd started earlier and never finished. Good thing I'd seen it before, because it was hard to concentrate. My mind churned through the details of Monday night. Dolores. The man running down the stairs. The man snooping around my property. The open window. The blood on the wall. The overflowing bathtub. Even the tally marks I'd found on Violet's computer, which could have been irrelevant to the case, but it was hard to overlook anything at this point. Stormy said Violet ate healthy. The tally marks could have been calories eaten, the number of Twinkies she'd consumed, the number of people she'd ticked off that day and wanted to kill her...

Kevin smacked my thigh, and I jumped. "Your phone." He held it up to my face. Amy's name flashed across the screen. "Does this thing ever *not* ring?"

"No." I shook my head, hoping to clear the thoughts of Violet so I wouldn't sound anxious when I answered. But my brain is not an Etch A Sketch, and Amy knew me too well.

"What's wrong?" she immediately asked.

"Nothing. What's wrong with you? It's really late there."

"I was about to go to sleep when I received this concerning text message. Why are you bringing Tom to New York? What happened with Chase?"

"What are you talking about? I'm bringing Chase."

"According to this text from Tom, he'll be accompanying you to New York."

"What!" I bolted upright and knocked the ice cream out of Kevin's hand. It landed on the carpet in a chocolate and banana blob. Kevin went to the kitchen to get a towel while I stood there, blubbering profanity under my breath. Tom had crossed the line.

"I'm going to text Tom right now and say he's not going," Amy said.

"No, don't do that."

"Cambria Jane Clyne, I *am* going to text him," Amy said.

I pictured her face puce and her jaw clenched. She only used my full name when she was mad.

"You've spent way too many years waiting for this guy to get his act together. I've watched you cry over him, pine over him. Daydream about your family being together. Hell, I've watched you lie to your parents, let them believe he's gay just so they won't think he's a player who stomped on your heart. Which *he* did. This isn't one of those romance novels where the super hot, playboy baby daddy changes. He's not interested in a relationship, but he doesn't want another man in Lilly's life, so he's marking his territory. He might as well pee on you! How many times has he attempted to start something with you and ultimately pulled away?" She didn't wait for my answer. "Too many times. He doesn't want to be with you. Listen to me, Cambria. I love you. I always have. I always will. Which is why I am telling you this. You have a very nice, very *attractive*, very *into* you boyfriend. Don't screw it up by giving into the *what ifs* with Tom. If you let him, he'll string you along for the rest of your lives."

...Um...

I stood there like I was carved of flesh, with the phone at my ear and Kevin at my feet, scrubbing ice cream out of the carpet. I was going to say, "No, don't text Tom. I'll take care of it." I didn't want her wasting energy on my mess, not when she should be focusing on dancing, but *geez*.

"I'll send you Chase's information," I said, my voice small.

"Good! No more getting toyed with. You're beyond that, Cambria."

Yeah, I know was what I thought. "Thanks for the pep talk" was what I said, to make her feel better.

We hung up, and I ran my hands down my face, feeling exhausted and still sore from the night before. Why everyone suddenly felt the need to point out my personal flaws was beyond me.

"What was that about?" Kevin walked the ice cream–stained towel to the kitchen and tossed it into the sink.

I fell to the couch and dropped my head into my hands, feeling dizzy. "Baby daddy drama."

"I don't get your relationship."

"That makes two of us."

Kevin sat beside me and positioned a pillow behind his head. "I've never heard the story of how you guys got together."

"Do you really want to know? Or will I start the story and you'll roll your eyes and say you don't care?"

Kevin thought this over and decided, "Probably the latter. You're long-winded." He winked, and I couldn't help but smile. I'd learned to love Kevin's dry wit and cocky banter.

"The short version is, we met. We drank. We made Lilly. I told him I wanted a relationship. He said he didn't want one, though he doesn't recall ever having this conversation. He shoved me into the friend zone. Last year, he decided to take me out of the friend zone. We kissed in my bathroom the day after my birthday, but he pulled away. I don't think he would have given me a second thought if I hadn't gotten pregnant. Sometimes I wonder if I would have given him a second thought if I hadn't gotten pregnant. It's really hard not to have feelings for someone you created something so beautiful with. But Chase is wonderful and—"

"This is the short version?" Kevin interrupted

Did I say I loved Kevin's dry wit and cocky banter?

I meant *tolerated.*

"Fine," I said, "Tom's a player. Always has been. Always will be. I'm happy with Chase. The end."

"Interesting. I always thought it was him who was more into you than the other way around," said Kevin.

"What would make you think that?" I asked.

"Because he represented me as a favor to you, and I wasn't an easy client."

True. He fired Tom via email.

"He's always around even if it's not his day with Lilly," Kevin continued. "He planned a birthday surprise for you...didn't he take a bullet for you, too?"

"Yes."

"Have you ever taken a bullet for him?"

"No." I would, though. I think. "He obviously cares for me deeply, but whenever we get close, he pulls away and finds solace with another woman."

"Ouch."

"It hurt for the first couple of years. Now I have Chase. I've never had anything like this before either. He's wonderful." A pang of loneliness stabbed at my heart. I missed him.

The baritone ding-dong of the lobby door filled my apartment, and Kevin and I exchanged a look.

"Are you expecting anyone?" he asked.

"Not that I know of."

CHAPTER THIRTEEN

———

—I can be a little obsessive.

The outside lobby doorbell rang three more times before I was able to answer. Stormy stood on the other side of the door, holding a vase filled with beautiful yellow flowers. "Sorry to bother you. I came to drop these off before I go home for the night." She shot her arms out, and a bit of water spilled onto the brick below. "It's for you. Peruvian Lilies represent friendship and devotion." She unleashed a grin, baring oversized teeth. "I *googled* that."

I took the flowers and inhaled their sweet scent. "So you got your icons back?"

"Mmmhmmm. I also showed an apartment and maybe even rented it." She sounded so proud of herself that I couldn't help but smile.

"Congratulations. I knew you could do it." Actually, that was a lie. I was almost positive she'd accidentally burn down the building. Not that I had room to judge when it came to burning down buildings.

"I wouldn't have been able to do it without you," she said.

True. "Have you heard any word on Violet?"

Her face paled. "Not one word from anyone! Heaven help her." She stopped to cross herself. "The police took her computer shortly after you left. Maybe they'll find something on there."

I thought about the tally marks and wondered what Hampton made of them.

"Then a group of men and women with gloves on, and blue jackets, and ugly man shoes, went through her desk, too," Stormy continued.

I felt a whoosh of panic, thinking of my fingerprints smudged all over her personal things.

Please, please don't let my snooping compromise evidence.

Stormy continued to talk while I worked through a slight panic attack. "Caused quite a frenzy around the community," she said. "I think residents are beginning to suspect that Violet isn't on vacation."

I wet my lips, feeling a bit lightheaded. "It might help for everyone to know the truth. A resident could have seen someone suspicious." Which reminded me of Clint Eastwood. "Can you come in for a minute? I want to show you something."

"Pfft!" Stormy waved her hand as if I were being ridiculous. "Honey, I have more than a minute. I have no life. Just you wait."

I let her in and offered her a seat on the comfy lobby couch while I fetched the drawing, but she followed me instead. "What a lovely office!" she said as we squeezed past my desk. "Goodness, and your apartment is so close. You've got the best commute in all of Los Angeles!" she said when I opened the door to my kitchen. "And would you look at that! Job comes with a *man*." She growled when she saw Kevin lying on my couch in nothing but holey shorts and ice cream dribbling down his chest. "Aren't you the *hunky* monkey?"

Kevin gave me a who-the-hell-is-this-woman look.

"Kevin, this is Stormy. Stormy, Kevin," I said.

Stormy placed her hand over her heart. "Pleased to make your acquaintance, Kevin. You got a hottie here." Stormy cocked a thumb in my direction. "You're a lucky man."

Kevin and I exchanged a look. Neither of us was in the mood to correct her, so I showed her the sketch. "Do you know who this is?"

She tapped her finger to her chin. "He looks familiar, but not like someone I've seen in person before, more like someone I've seen on the television."

"Like Clint Eastwood," I said.

She shook her head. "Not so much. Gosh, this man looks so familiar. Where have I seen him before? Is he a model?"

Model?

Model...

Model!

Crap!

I felt an almighty heave of horror.

Fox!

Crap. Crap. Crap. Crap.

I'd been so consumed with Violet and helping Stormy with her job that I'd completely forgotten to do my own. I should have had Fox's application processed and a deposit collected yesterday. No doubt he'd already found an apartment in a neighboring building by now—one that was gluten-free.

Note to self: you're an idiot.

"You OK?" Stormy had a hand on my shoulder.

"I'm fine." My tone was harsher than I'd intended. It wasn't her fault that I'd dropped the ball. "I just remembered I have something I need to do right now," I said more sweetly this time, hoping she wouldn't think me rude.

Based on Stormy's expression: mission *not* accomplished.

"If I'm bothering you, then I should be leaving," she said, except she didn't move. Instead, she stood next to the kitchen table with a hand on each hip and her mouth set to a line.

Great, I'd offended Stormy.

"I'm not rushing you out," I tried to explain. "It was just that—"

"We were having sex!" Kevin said loud enough for the neighbors to hear, and I nearly fell over.

He's officially lost his mind.

I was about to adamantly protest, but the left side of Stormy's mouth twitched upward. "Excusez-moi. Let me leave you two alone." She fanned herself. I felt my face go red. "I don't want to ruin the mood."

I couldn't formulate a coherent sentence, so I said nothing and walked Stormy out.

She stopped at the door to give this lovely tidbit of advice: "Get it while you can, girl. When you get to be my age, men don't have the stamina to keep it up."

Gross.

Stormy stepped out into the hot night air. "Would you please let me know if they tell you anything about Violet?" I asked.

"Of course I will." She folded her arms. "And you let me know if you hear anything, too."

I leaned against the doorjamb. "Have you talked to the owners or her daughter?"

"No on the daughter. I sent the owners the vacancy report, but I haven't heard anything back." She chewed on her lip. "I hope I did it right. All I did was send them the list Antonio gave me."

"I'm curious why Violet would tell me you had twelve vacancies if you really had three." I was still stuck on this. "Also, why it showed twelve vacancies in Panda. That should be updated, especially if you don't keep hard copy records."

"Must have been a mistake." She shrugged. "Like I said, Violet had been struggling these past few weeks."

Good point.

Still.

I couldn't stop thinking about the discrepancy in vacancies. No matter how hard I tried. Even after I said good night to Stormy. Even after I sat beside Kevin on the couch. Even after we finished *If Only* and started another episode. No matter how hard I tried, the thought wormed its way back into my mind. Managers don't lie and say they have more vacancies than they really do. They just don't. Why would we? It made us look bad. Who wants to look bad in front of other managers? Not me.

Unless the lie benefitted her.

But how?

Why would carrying more vacancies benefit her? Patrick had mentioned the owners recently asked how long vacancies should sit. Which meant they were concerned. Which meant they had vacant units sitting. Three vacancies in a 255-unit place isn't terrible. It's great, actually. The list on Panda wasn't right, obviously, since it had listed Apartment 105...

I give up!

"Where are you going? It's almost ten," Kevin said.

I slipped on my shoes and threw Einstein up into a knot at the top of my head. "There's something fishy going on next door."

"Yeah, the manager's missing."

I rolled my eyes. "Beside that. There's a discrepancy in their vacancies and..." I could tell I'd already lost Kevin. "Stay here. I'll be right back."

"Not your monkey!" I heard him yell as I closed the door.

True. Not my monkey. Not my circus. And maybe the discrepancy in vacancies was an oversight. Or maybe it was a clue to Violet's disappearance.

Or maybe I should just stick to running my own circus.

Either way, I marched to Cedar Creek, typed in the code Dolores gave me, and pulled open the whimsical doors, climbed the stairs to the third floor, found Apartment 306—one of the apartments on the original Panda list—and knocked.

CHAPTER FOURTEEN

———

—And by a little obsessive, I mean a lot.

No answer.

Which meant one of two things: no one was home, or the apartment was vacant, 105 was an oversight in the system, and I'd walked over there for nothing.

Except…

I placed my ear against the door. Two people, presumably men, based on the deep tone of their voices, were having a conversation. About what? I couldn't tell. They were muffled through the expensive wood.

I raised my fist and gave the door three more taps using my knuckles. The mumbling stopped. Footsteps approached. The door opened enough for me to see a black sofa, white drapes, a rustic coffee table, and a slender man with oversized glasses and a cardigan on.

Guess it's not vacant.

"I know you!" The cardigan man pointed, and I turned around. No one was behind me, so he must have been talking to me, except I'd never seen this man before. "You work here," he said in a way that insinuated this was not a good thing.

"Uh…no."

"Yes you do." He cradled a large wineglass filled to the brim. "I saw you sitting at Violet's desk earlier. I have a bone to pick with you. Wait there." He disappeared, and for whatever reasons (curiosity, need to please, the inability to properly use my brain), I waited. He returned with a piece of a paper and shoved it into my hands. It was a rental increase notification dated the day before Violet disappeared. "I've lived here four months, and my rent is increasing already. That's unconstitutional!"

Not unconstitutional, just bad business.

I read through the notification more thoroughly. Per the increase, this man's name was Frank, and his rent was now two hundred and fifty dollars more a month, unless he was willing to sign a one-year lease—then his rent would stay the same. No wonder he was upset. "Were you offered a move-in special upon signing?" I asked, trying to understand why Violet would give such an ultimatum to a new resident.

"I was *never* offered a special. This is just bad business!" He slurped his wine.

Embossed on the top of the paper was the Star Management Inc. logo—five silver stars circled around an *S*. I could have sworn Patrick had said the owners of Cedar Creek didn't use a management company. He was obviously mistaken. Star Management handled thousands of residential and commercial properties all over the country. I'd run across their name many times while doing resident verification...

Crap!

Resident verification!

I'd completely forget about Fox's application—*again!*

Note to self: do your own job!

I gave the notification back to Frank. "I'm sorry, but I'm unable to help you."

Frank blinked his eyes slowly, exaggerating the movements. "Then *why* are you here?"

Good question.

One I didn't have an answer to—not a logical one anyway.

Frank slurped his wine and rolled his eyes so far back into his head I was fairly certain he saw brain. "This place is run by morons." He slammed the door shut.

So, turned out Apartment 306 was not vacant.

I had no idea how this was pertinent, and Violet was still gone. I'd accomplished absolutely nothing.

Nada.

Zilch.

Zero.

My phone buzzed from my back pocket, and I checked to see who it was. Heat rose to my cheeks when I saw Tom's name. I'd forgotten about the text he'd sent Amy. I'd forgotten how upset I was with him. Missing apartment managers with inaccurate vacancy reports has a way of hogging your attention.

I leaned against the wall and lowered down to my butt, debating if I should answer or not. Problem was, no matter how much I didn't want to talk to him (and I really didn't), he was still the father of my child. So I answered, "What is wrong with you?"

"That's a loaded question."

"Why did you tell Amy you were coming to New York instead of Chase? She needs to focus all her energy on dancing, not your inability to listen to me."

"I didn't say *instead* of Chase."

"So the three of us will go together? That sounds fun."

"It could be."

I strangled the phone with both hands. He was still talking when I hit *End*. Frustrated, I beat the back of my head against the wall. I did this for awhile, until Frank opened the door and poked his head out. "What is that tapping?" He looked down and rolled his eyes. "I'm surrounded by morons."

True.

So true.

He flung the door shut, and I stood up slowly and walked toward the stairwell exit. I stopped at the window at the end of the hall and peered out, heaving a sigh. My breath fogged the glass, and I used the bottom of my shirt to wipe it clean. From three stories up, I had a perfect view of my community. The underwater lights illuminated the pool. Mickey was making his rounds. Silvia was in her nightie, checking the mail, with Harold on her shoulder. The kitchen light was on in Daniella's apartment. She never did call me back about the Eastwood look-a-like. Not completely unlike her. She typically only spoke to me when she was upset—which was quite often.

Everything appeared so normal, and yet something felt so off.

The Cedar Creeks parking gate slid open, and a silver Honda with a bright Hollywood Pizza sign on the roof pulled into an open visitors' spot along the wall, right beside the reserved maintenance parking. The deliveryman stepped out of his car, fixed his pants, picked at his teeth, ran a hand through his hair, and locked his Honda over his shoulder, using a key fob.

My first thought: *Hollywood Pizza delivers here!*

My second thought: *that deliveryman looks familiar.*

Tall, slender, and a lot like Bob Saget.

CHAPTER FIFTEEN

———

—Property management requires a surprisingly large amount of stalking.

Hampton answered on the third ring. "Yes, Cambria?" His words were laced with forced patience.

"I found Bob Saget." I practically flew down the stairs, going three at a time, holding tight to the railing as I neared the first floor. My foot slipped on a step, and I tumbled the rest of the way.

"What happened?" Now Hampton's voice was now laced with concern.

"Nothing. I'm fine." I stood and fell against the push bar to open the door. Adrenaline slammed against my chest as I searched the lobby. I hoped to make it down before the man had a chance to call for the elevator.

But I didn't see him.

With the phone still at my ear, I limped around, barely noticing the pain shooting down my leg. How that thing was still attached to my body was a miracle.

I rounded the corner and quickly retreated, plastering my back against the wall. "I found him," I whispered to Hampton and peeked my head around. The Bob Saget look-a-like stood at the Wow Fridge, taking in his choices.

"What's he doing?" Hampton asked in an equally hushed tone.

"He's grabbing a Gatorade and a bag of Lays from the fridge."

"Why are Lays in the fridge?"

"It's part of the *wow* factor."

The man ripped open his chips with his teeth and walked down the hallway. He didn't have a pizza or delivery bag on him, and his hat was shoved under his armpit. I watched as he passed the elevator. I watched as he passed the stairwell. I watched as he used the backside of his pants to wipe the grease off his hand. I watched as he knocked on an apartment door.

He waited and licked his fingertips clean one by one, until the door opened and he was granted entrance. I waited for the door to shut before I raised the phone to my ear and said, "He just entered Apartment 105. Dolores Rocklynn."

"I'll be right there."

CHAPTER SIXTEEN

———

—Stalking can get boring.

I kept an eye on Apartment 105 from my post at the end of the hall. I lay on the floor with a bag of Fritos open on my lap and my phone in my hand, texting Kevin. Lilly was still asleep, and he was on his second pint of ice cream.

There was a time, not too long ago, when I'd never allow Kevin in my apartment, let alone near my child. That was back when he was high and naked and a generally unpleasant person. Kevin was now clean and clothed and mostly pleasant.

"People change for two reasons," my Grandma Ruthie used to say. "Either their eyes have been opened, or their hearts have been broken. If we refuse to see the change in people and forgive, then we're only denying ourselves."

I was glad I'd given Kevin a second chance. With Amy gone, he'd become my stand-in best friend.

Once again, Grandma Ruthie knew what she was talking about. I missed that woman. She was a walking inspirational quote. The kind you see on Pinterest with the tree in the background or an ocean wave. I wondered what she would say about Tom. If she'd think he was indeed capable of changing. Or what she'd think about my mother's declaration about Lilly needing a sibling...

Ugh.

I pushed the bag of chips aside. No longer hungry. The thought of screwing up Lilly kept me up at night. I could picture her in twenty years, lying on a chaise lounge with an arm draped over her eyes. A therapist sitting on a high-backed velvet chair, dubiously taking notes as Lilly goes on and on and *on* about life

with her neurotic mother. Her childhood filled with tagging
along on property tours and sitting in small offices, being forced
to color all day while Mom worked.

Or…

I pictured her ending up just like me.

They say the apple doesn't fall far from the tree. Heaven
knew there were times I could *hear* my own mother coming out
of my mouth.

Not that growing up to be just like me would be horrible.
I was happy. Sure, my baby daddy had become a walking ulcer,
but he was a wonderful father and I *did* have a level-headed
boyfriend. I had a job that offered both a roof over our heads and
somewhat financial security. Yes, I had been shot at, taken
hostage, and arrested. I was also sitting on the floor of a fancy
high-rise waiting for the police to show up.

Also, the top button of my jeans may or may not have
been unbuttoned.

OK, so maybe my life wasn't all rainbows and
butterflies, but I was content.

Super content.

I wanted better than contentment for my child, though. I
wanted her to grow up to be more confident than me. More
coordinated. More intelligent. I wanted her to graduate from
college. I wanted her to o*wn* the building, not manage it. I
wanted her to have a child with a man who loved her back. I
wanted more for her, but I had no idea how to make sure that
happened.

Then I thought about Violet's daughter, who grew up in
similar circumstances and was thriving. Which brought my mind
back to Violet and the Bob Saget look-a-like hiding out in
Apartment 105. I checked the time on my phone. Hampton was
either diddle-daddling around or was on the other side of LA
when he'd gotten my call. Either way, almost an hour had gone
by since he'd said, "I'll be *right* there."

I shifted to my side and stared at the whimsical doors,
willing them to open, willing Hampton to walk in, willing him to
hurry up!

The doors opened. Except it wasn't Hampton. It was a thin man holding a Trader Joe's bag, talking on his phone. A woman slipped in behind him...

Holy crap!

It was the woman from the police station, the one who gave me judgy eyes. I'd recognize her anywhere. She had on the same leopard print leotard, her light hair the size of Canada, and a ferret on a leash.

I tried not to stare, but, I mean, she was walking a ferret, and her leotard was about two sizes too small, revealing every little nook and cranny.

She peeked into the office, cupping her hands against the glass, leaving two large smudge marks. She tried the door a few times, but it was locked. "Dammit," she muttered under her breath and pulled a cigarette from her cleavage.

I loudly cleared my throat.

The woman spun around. "Can I help you?"

"You're not allowed to smoke in here."

"Oh yeah?" She shoved the cigarette between her lips and pulled a lighter from her cleavage. I wondered what else she had in there. "Says who?"

"California."

"Yeah, well, don't you worry your pretty little head. My mom runs the joint, and I can smoke if I want."

"Is your mom Stormy?" I asked.

She lit the cigarette and puffed out a circle. "Nah. Violet Pumpkin. She's the manager and has been for a long while."

"Wh-wh...hold on. Wait...wait. You're Violet's daughter?"

"Yeah, what's it to you?"

"B-b-but." *Breathe, Cambria.* "Did you just get here from Florida?"

"Florida?" She took another drag and dropped her cigarette on the ground and put it out with the toe of her slip-on heels. "I came from Hollywood."

"So you must have a sister that lives in Florida?" I asked, trying to understand.

"No sister. Only child. Trust me. My mom couldn't handle more than one." She walked her ferret past me and toward the elevator.

"Hold on." I stood, buttoned the top of my pants, and ran after her. "What college did you go to?"

"Look, sweetie, I don't know who you are, but you're starting to get on my nerves." She slammed the *Call* button.

The elevator doors parted, and I jumped in front of the woman, blocking her from entering. "What college did you attend?" I asked again.

"Step aside, sweetie, before I remove you myself."

I stood firm. This woman was an imposter, and I was not about to let her get away with it. "You are not Violet's daughter," I said as the doors closed behind me. "Her daughter lives in Florida, went to UCLA, has two kids, and a husband."

The woman curled her lip. "What the hells are you talking about? My mother only had one kid. That's all she had time for, and I don't have no husband in Florida. I got a few ex-husbands in Arizona and one in Nevada, but not Florida. I don't do humidity. Ain't good for my hair."

"You're lying," I said and squeezed my eyes shut, pretty sure this woman was about to deck me.

When the blow didn't come, I peeked one eye open, but she was gone. *No!* I heard the stairwell door slam shut and started to chase after her, when someone grabbed me by the arm and pulled me back. And that someone was Hampton.

Finally!

"What took you so long?" I snapped, yanking my arm free.

"Hello to you too."

"Sorry. *Hello.* What took you so long?"

"I was on the other side of town. Why are you chasing after Violet's daughter?"

I threw up in my mouth a little. "That can't be her daughter. I saw that woman at the police station yesterday."

"She was there to see me."

"B-b-but, I talked to Violet on Monday. She told me about her daughter and grandkids. That's not the daughter Violet described!"

"That *is* her daughter, and she has five kids, but they've never met Violet. They all live with their fathers."

"Wh...wh...no. That can't be right. Violet said her daughter lived in Florida and has two kids, a good job, and was a normal member of society... Why are you shaking your head?"

Hampton took a step closer. I could smell In-N-Out on his breath, which made me both angry and hungry. Did he stop for a burger when he should have been here questioning the guy in Apartment 105? "Between you and me," he started, "the two have a bit of a tumultuous relationship. They went ten years without speaking and only recently reconnected. The daughter moved out when she was seventeen and was on the streets for a few years, until she got clean. Now she lives in Hollywood and works at a bowling alley. We've found no record of another child. Just the one daughter, Hollow."

Hollow?

No wonder they had a strained relationship. I'd have issues with my mother too if she named me *Hollow* Pumpkin.

"Why would Violet lie to me?" I asked, feeling a bit faint. "There was no reason to."

"You're not the only one she lied to. Several people we interviewed told us the same story. Seemed Violet liked to tell tales."

You could have knocked me over with a feather. "When you say the daughter was on the streets, do you mean..."

Please say sleeping.

"She was a prostitute."

Of course she was! I threw my hands up in the air and made a small circle. My single thread of hope for Lilly had been snapped. More than snapped. It had been snapped, tossed in the fire, and charred into an unrecognizable pile of ash.

First Violet lied about her daughter.

Then she lied about the vacancies.

But why?

How did lying to me benefit her? It didn't make any sense.

"If the two had such a terrible relationship, why is Hollow here right now?" I asked.

"She told us that she would stop by to water the plants."

I gave Hampton a look. "And you're buying that? Who's to say she had nothing to do with Violet's disappearance?"

"We're verifying her alibi." He put a hand on the small of my back, willing me forward. "Right now let's concentrate on your Stairwell Guy. Come on."

Right. Bob Saget. I'd almost forgotten.

Hampton and I took the ten-foot journey to Apartment 105 in silence. Me still processing. Him adjusting his hair. Hampton knocked on the door, and Dolores answered. She had on bright pink legging with fish printed on them. "Can I help you?"

"Sorry to bother you at this hour, ma'am," Hampton said. I stood behind him, still reeling from the daughter revelation. "Not sure if you remember me from the other night. My name is Detective Hampton." He held up his badge, and concern flashed across Dolores's face. "Do you have anyone else living here that fits this description?" He held up the sketch.

Dolores squinted at the drawing. "He looks similar to my son, but he doesn't live here. He visits often." She turned around. "David!" The Hollywood Pizza deliveryman appeared from the kitchen, eating Chinese takeout from the carton with chopsticks.

"What's wrong?" Up close, David looked more like Bob Saget's close relative. His hair was shorter. His arms were covered in sleeve tattoos, and he had the tiniest bit of chest hair peeking out over the top of his shirt.

Hampton dove into questions, not skipping a beat. "Were you here the night Violet Pumpkin was discovered missing?"

"Yeah. It was the same night we had a leak in my mom's bathroom."

"Where were you when I was questioning your mother?" Hampton asked.

"Yeah, no. Look, man." David put down the takeout and extended his arms, crossing his wrists. "If you're going to arrest me, just get it over with."

"Stop that!" Dolores pushed his hands down. "He did nothing wrong. He was with me all night."

"Why would I arrest you?" Hampton asked, his face remaining stoic.

"Yeah, no. Look, man, we tried to get a hold of Violet, and she wasn't answering. So I ran upstairs and kicked the door in, tried to turn off the water, saw her personal items on the counter, the toilet paper holder on the floor, and her closet torn apart. I called my mom, and she told me to get the hell out of there. That's the truth, and I'm sticking to it."

I watched the exchange over Hampton's shoulder—my eyes bounced between the two men as they continued.

Hampton: Why were you in the closet?

David: I heard a noise in there, but when I walked in, no one was there.

Hampton: Why did you run away if you had nothing to hide?

David: Yeah, no. Man, I don't want to get involved. I still don't.

Hampton: Did you know Violet Pumpkin?

David: I did some business with her, but I didn't hurt her. Not my style.

Hampton: What business?

David: If you want to ask more questions, then I'm getting a lawyer.

I had no idea what to make of David's demeanor. He stood there casually, like he and Hampton were chatting about the latest Dodgers game.

Dolores interjected. "Violet was not a good person. We've lived here less than four months, and she's already given us a rental increase unless we sign a year lease."

"Giving out rental increases doesn't make her a bad person," I said, and everyone snapped their heads in my direction, as if suddenly realizing I was there.

I went back to my spot and clasped my hands together. Until a thought trotted into my head. "Was the window opened or closed?" I asked David.

"What window?" Dolores asked.

"The window in the closet." I looked at David. "You said you heard a noise. Was the window in the closet open or closed?"

"Closed."

Oh hell.

If David was telling the truth, and I had no idea if he was—apparently I was a horrible judge of liars—then someone opened the window in the ten minutes between when David left and Antonio and I arrived.

"I'm not answering another question without my lawyer present." David picked up his takeout and slurped a noodle.

"Looks like we'll have to speak later." Hampton wrapped his hand around my bicep, forcing me forward.

"What are you doing?" I asked. "Don't you want to question him more?"

"Keep walking," he muttered.

I looked over my shoulder. Dolores and I locked eyes, and she extended her middle finger then ran it across her neck.

Um...yikes!

Hampton yanked me through the lobby with more force than was warranted, mumbling something under his breath. "Let me go," I protested. "I can walk on my own."

He waited until we passed through the whimsical doors before he released my arm, leaving three red spots from where his fingers were.

"Using physical force is not necessary," I said.

Hampton ran his hands down his face, still mumbling.

"What is wrong?" I demanded.

Hampton pointed to the building. "I should have never let you come to the door with me. I could have brought David down to the station and had you identify him in a lineup if needed." He exhaled and squeezed his eyes shut. "That was stupid of me, and I'm sorry."

"You don't need to apologize, Hampton. I'm a big girl who can make stupid decisions all by myself. So you think David is the one who took Violet?"

"I think David knows something. I think he looks familiar. I think there's a reason he didn't want to be questioned on Monday night. I think we're going to bring him down and have him questioned. I think you identifying him brought us one step closer to finding out what happened to Violet. I think Cruller is going to *kill* me when he finds out about this."

"Does he need to know?" I asked.

"You don't keep secrets from your partner."

Sound advice.

Made me think about the kiss Tom and I shared in my bathroom a few months back. I never did tell Chase. In my defense, I didn't consider us serious at the time.

I had a sinking suspicion this was going to backfire on me.

But I could only deal with one potential disaster at a time. "What are we going to do about David?"

"*I* am going to call in for backup, and we're going to bring him down for questioning. *You* are going home."

"H-home?" I stuttered. "Will you at least let me know if he's been arrested? I think his mom wants to kill me now."

Hampton placed a hand on my shoulder. "I'll keep you in the loop as much as I can." He smiled. I think it was the first time I'd seen his teeth.

We were having a moment, Hampton and I. It was nice.

Poor guy. He must be lonely, I thought, what with no wife and no dog to keep him company.

The little light bulb in my head turned on.

"Have you ever seen *The Little Mermaid*?" I asked.

He dropped his hand. "Yes, why?"

"What do you think of Ursula? Evil aside, she's hot. Right? Because I may have someone in mind for you if you're ready to date."

"OK." He walked off.

Perhaps *OK* was Hampton's version of *goodbye*?

The whimsical door opened, and Hollow came out, holding a cardboard box piled high with succulents, and trinkets, and picture frames, and toilet paper. Her ferret was at her side— its little legs struggling to keep up. Hollow's face was hidden behind the box, but I could see the smoke and smell the nicotine as she passed by, her heels clanking on the ground, much like Lilly's dress-up shoes did.

A red truck pulled up to the curb. A bone-thin man with no shirt on leaned over and pushed open the passenger-side door. "Hurry the hell up, woman. I got places to be."

Hollow dropped the box into the back of the truck, picked up her ferret, and as soon as her leopard print butt landed on the seat, the truck took off, before the door had even closed.

Oh hell.
I need four Advil and a tub of ice cream.

CHAPTER SEVENTEEN

———

—You can tell if a prospective resident will be good or a royal pain in the butt just by looking at their social media profile pictures.

It was midnight when I fell into bed and pulled a pillow over my head. Sleep was impossible. Whenever I closed my eyes, Violet's face appeared. I lay in a dark room, staring at the ceiling, hot and sweaty, the fan spinning on low, with Lilly kicking me in the kidney every three minutes.

The timing of Violet's disappearance, the lie about her daughter, the rental increases, vacancy discrepancies, David, Dolores, Hampton's toupee—it all spun around and around and around in my mind like a washer stuck on the speed cycle.

The first call from Dolores came at 8:15 PM.

David would have exited Violet's apartment around 9:55 PM, which meant he entered around 9:45 PM. The window was closed. When I entered shortly after David exited, the window was open. I was stuck on this. Why would he open the window if he wasn't going to go out it? It didn't make sense. I believed someone went out the window between the time David left and Antonio and I arrived. Did that someone go out the window with Violet? Was it possible to escape through a window two stories up with a dead body and go unnoticed?

Of course, David could be a liar.

Like Violet.

Which begged the question, was it Violet who went out the window? Was it easier to run away than deal with the lies she'd told?

When the clock struck seven, my upstairs neighbor, Mickey, hurled himself out of bed and thumped across my ceiling, and I gave up. Regardless of what had happened with Violet, and David, and the window, and Dolores, I had a job to do. And I hadn't been doing it well. Taking care of my family had to be priority one.

I took a shower *and* shaved my legs. Ate a hearty breakfast of Pop-Tarts and a banana— then Lilly and I headed to Burbank. We found a parking spot two blocks away this time, and the temp had dipped to a manageable range.

Things were starting to look up.

Of course, I still had to deal with the aftermath of rental increases and the infractions I'd passed out on Tuesday.

Lilly and I stood behind the mailboxes, and I peeked into the courtyard before I dared enter, hoping no one was waiting with pitchforks and flaming torches.

Or worse, notices to vacate.

"Oh my word." I brought my hand to my mouth, barely able compute what my eyes were seeing.

Lilly tugged on my shirt. "What's wrong, Mommy?"

"Everything is...done." No wet towels hung over the railing. No trash outside the door. No furniture on the walkway. No cardboard in the windows. It was...*clean*.

I spun around in a slow circle, with my arms out, like Julie Andrews about to burst into song. Patrick was right. "An iron fist!"

"Is that like Iron Man?"

"Pretty much." I unlocked my office door and pushed it open "Your mom is basically a superhero—oh for the love!"

The teenagers were at it again.

I covered Lilly's eyes and quickly ushered her outside. The teens bolted out of my office and ran away, pulling on their clothes as they left.

"What were them doing?" Lilly asked.

"*They* were, uh, dancing."

"Like a sexy man shimmy?"

Heaven help me. I'm screwing up my child.

"Mommy, why are you hitting yourself in the forehead like that?"

"No reason...um...here's an idea." I dug around in my bag and pulled out a Tupperware container filled with rice and little farm animals—an idea I'd found on Pinterest.

Lilly gave me a mom-has-finally-lost-her-mind look. "Do I eat this?"

"No. It's a sensory activity. Dig around in the rice and find all the animals."

Lilly stared at me like I'd just produced a container of poo. "Can me have your phone instead?"

"It's *I*, and no." I unfolded a metal chair in the corner of my office and plopped Lilly down with her rice. "Have fun."

I bleached the sperm-taminated area then got to work. I unfolded my own chair and unloaded my bag. Lilly had both hands in the rice container and pulled a little sheep out.

I mentally gave myself a pat on the back.

See, you're a good parent. Lilly will be just fine.

I, however, would not be. Not if I didn't process the application for Fox, pronto. I scanned the paperwork using an app on my phone and emailed it to Patrick, praying he wouldn't notice the date on the bottom.

Once the application was safely in Patrick's inbox, I opened my laptop and connected to the internet (my phone was a hot spot, because I'm fancy like that. Also, Patrick paid for it). I conducted my usual prospective resident investigation. Starting with all social media accounts: Facebook, Instagram, Snapchat, and Twitter. Fox's smolder and washboard abs were on all of them. He even had an IMDb account. His most recent role was two months ago as Dead Guy #6 in an episode of *If Only*.

Which was more impressive than a rental magazine.

Based on all his social media accounts, Fox didn't appear to be a drug dealer, or a party animal, or crazy, and that was about all I cared about.

Time to do the resident verification.

I called his current landlord.

"Liberty Park Apartments, this is Stanley."

"My name is Cambria Clyne, and I'm calling from Elder Property Management. I have a rental verification for your resident in Apartment 412, named—"

"I know Fox."

FYI: not a good sign.

"Can I send over a rental verification form?" I asked.

"We're not able to give out any information about residents aside from rent amount. Company policy."

That's code for:

A) This resident has been given notice to vacate, but I can't tell you that, because then he'll possibly sue me. Or:

B) This resident pays his rent on time but is a royal pain in my rear.

My rear already had plenty of pains, but Burbank had plenty of vacancies. "At the very least, I need to verify he lives there. I have a signed rental application I can send," I said.

"If you go to our website, there's an online form you can submit. It's Star Management Inc. dot com backslash Liberty Park."

I froze. "You work for Star Management Inc.?" Dumb question. He just said he did. So I followed it up with, "Do you know anything about the place Star manages off Sepulveda?"

"Palmwood Park?"

"No."

"Seashore Park?"

"No."

"Rosewood Park?"

I was sensing a pattern.

As Stanley talked, I looked up the Star Management website and searched through the properties listed. Every building in the Southern California region had "Park" in the title. Even a Seagull Park located in Santa Monica. An unfortunate name choice. Seagulls crapped everywhere and stole your food—not an animal I would want associated with my apartment building.

In short, all *Parks* and no *Creeks*.

Unless I was missing something. "Does Star manage a place called Cedar Creek?" I asked.

"No," said Stanley, and my head imploded.

"Are you sure? Could it have been a newly acquired property?"

"No. I'm the district manager, helping out today because my PM is on maternity leave."

This meant two things:

1) Stanley was well acquainted of all Star rental properties in the area.

2) Out of the thousands of residents he was over, he still knew Fox by apartment number and first name only.

Not a great sign.

"If you submit the form within the next ten minutes, I can get it back to you right away."

"I will, thank you." I hung up, slid the phone down from my cheek slowly, and stared at the website. The company logo, the five small golden stars in a circle around an *S*, the same logo on the rental increase. Well, except for the color. Cedar Creek's rental increase had silver stars. Unless there were two Star Management companies?

I googled *Star Management* and…nope, only one.

Next, I googled *Violet Pumpkin Los Angeles, California* and got over 5,588,000 results.

Geez.

I skimmed through the first one hundred pages. The top hits were her private social media accounts, Cedar Creek's Facebook page, website, and roughly twenty different bakeries that offered pumpkin pie.

At the bottom of page ninety-five, one hit caught my eye:

Fictitious Business Name—Los Angeles Flyer—Ad Pay—Legal Notices

The *Los Angeles Flyer* was a free magazine delivered on Thursdays. They'd come by and dump forty on my doorstep. I'd give most to Silvia so she could line the bottom of Harold's cage and left a few in the office for residents to grab. Which they never did.

I clicked on the link.

The ad you are looking for has expired or is no longer available.

I should have dropped it.

But I couldn't.

"Flyer's Ad department, this is Santiago," answered a man with a Spanish accent.

I could hear fingers typing away on keyboards in the background, like a busy news office. Which I found funny. The Flyer mostly ran fluff pieces, classified ads, and obituaries.

"Hello, my name is Cambria Clyne the apartment manager—" I caught myself. Some habits are hard to break. "I'm on your website trying to find an ad for a fictitious business name, but it says it's expired."

"When was the ad placed?"

I went back to my original search and read the description below the hit.

Fictitious Business Name—Los Angeles Flyer—Ad Pay—Legal Notices

May 11, 2011. Full Name of Registrant: Violet Marie Pumpkin. The business is conducted by an individual.

I relayed this information to Santiago.

"The ads are up on the website for thirty days only," he said.

"Is there any way you could look up the original order placed and let me know what the name of the business is?"

"Hold on." The line went silent, and I drummed my fingers on my laptop.

"Momma, can I be done now?" Lilly asked.

"Sure…ahhh!" Rice covered the floor, and Lilly had flipped the Tupperware container over and was using it as a hat. I sandwiched the phone between my shoulder and ear, grabbed the broom, and swept up the mess.

Santiago came back. "Superior Tenancy Apartment Rentals."

"Superior Tenancy Apartment Rentals," I repeated. What a mouthful. I imagined having to answer the phone, *Superior Tenancy Apartment Rentals, this is…*

I slowly lowered my arm to my side, phone still in hand, Santiago still talking. Lilly still wearing Tupperware, rice and farm animals still on floor.

The company acronym was STAR!

I hung up on Santiago, abandoned the broom, and went back to the laptop, my fingers shaking as they pounded around on the keyboard. The website for Cedar Creek filled my monitor, and I searched each tab, looking for the link to a management company.

But there wasn't one.

I didn't want to jump to conclusions…

CHAPTER EIGHTEEN

—But I did anyway...

"I believe Violet rented certain units under her own management company. She created Superior Tenancy Apartment Rentals so she could use the STAR acronym. That way, when a prospective resident looked up the management company, they'd see the *real* Star Management and assume they were the same. Star has a great reputation. She kept the rent money on those units for herself. The apartments are over four thousand dollars a month, which meant even if she had six or seven units, she was pulling in over twenty thousand dollars each month! Around the four-month mark, she'd pass out a rental increase giving residents the option to pay more or sign a lease for the same price. I bet the lease would be with the owners of the building! Violet didn't allow Stormy to do any of the management. She never trained her to use the software. And Antonio, the maintenance man, isn't in charge of turning vacant units. The owners don't get along with Violet and were looking for a reason to let her go, which is probably why they were doing an audit. Violet was about to be caught! It all makes perfect sense now!"

"And you figured this all out by doing a Google search?" Chase asked.

I switched the phone to my other ear. "Yes."

"Did you tell Hampton?"

"He didn't answer when I called." And I called several times. Like ten. "Where are you? I can barely hear you."

"I'm at the Vegas airport, standing in line about to board my connector flight home. Where are you?"

"We're standing in front of Cedar Creek."

I could almost hear Chase shaking his head. "Why?"

"Waiting. Stormy must be giving a tour, because she's not in the office. But it's not like I'm going to tell her what I suspect about Violet."

"Then why are you there, Cambria?"

"I want to find something to debunk my theory. Even if Violet lied about her daughter, I still respected her as a manager. I respected her career. She gave me something to aspire to." And I didn't aspire to be a liar and a thief.

"You tampering with evidence or inadvertently tipping someone off who is involved could severely damage this case." His voice was stern. He rarely used his stern voice. It was hot.

Note to self: Google how long the flight from Vegas to LAX is.

"Can we go home now?" Lilly pulled on my hand. "*Pleeeaaassseee.*"

"Tell Lilly I have a gift for her," Chase said.

I relayed the message to Lilly, and her eyes went wide. "When can me have it?"

"It's *I*, and when he gets home," I said.

Lilly puffed out her chest and jerked around in a circle. "What are you doing?" I asked.

"A sexy man shimmy!"

Oh geez.

"Did she just say 'sexy man shimmy'?" Chase asked.

I could hear the familiar swooshing and pinging sounds of the inside of the plane, and I pictured Chase pulling his suitcase down the narrow aisle, looking for his seat.

"She sure did." I placed a hand on Lilly's shoulder to stop her. Even though it looked less like a shimmy and more like an epileptic episode. If she sexy man shimmied in front of Tom, he'd have a heart attack.

"Thank you," Chase said to someone other than me. "Cambria, I just sat down, and I have a minute before we take off. Real quickly, I want to emphasize this. *Don't* talk to Stormy or Antonio right now. Try Hampton again, and if he doesn't answer, send him a text. He might be unable to answer his phone, but he should be able to read a text."

"Fine," I said. "We did find the guy who ran me down in the stairwell. His name is David Rocklynn. Ever heard of him?" Long shot. Los Angeles had almost four million residents. But before Chase worked as a detective, he worked undercover with the narcotics division and had met a lot of perps. He also loved Hollywood Pizza.

"Short hair. Early twenties. Sleeve tattoos. Looks like a young Bob Saget."

Dang. "Yes! How do you know him?"

"We've had a few run-ins. He works as a bookie. Taking illegal bets on everything from horse races to reality television."

Reality television?

I thought about the magazine in Violet's desk, with Raven's—the season's favorite to win—bio dog-eared and the - *100* written beside it. If Amy was this season's favored to go home first and had +2500, and Raven was this season's favored to win and was a -100, then minus must be good and plus must be bad. Violet went missing the night of the shocking elimination. Could she have placed a large bet on Raven, and when she was eliminated, David came looking for Violet, ready to collect his money. When she couldn't pay, he took her and she was currently being tortured or held at ransom until she's able to come up with the money?

Holy crap!

"I gotta go," I said. "Travel safe. Can't wait to see you. Bye." I hung up and composed a seven-paragraph text message that took three minutes for my phone to send to Hampton.

"Let's go." I grabbed Lilly by the hand and turned to leave.

"Yo, Cambria!" someone yelled, and I turned around to see who was calling my name. "Up here!"

I used my hand as a visor. Antonio was on a third floor balcony, waving. I waved. Lilly waved. We did this for awhile.

"You looking for Stormy?" he asked. "She's giving a tour."

"I was, but it's not important. I'll come by later."

Antonio leaned over and rested his elbows on the patio railing. "Did you hear the news? They arrested a guy in Apartment 105."

An arrest!

No wonder Hampton hadn't gotten back to me. Last I heard he was going to question David, not arrest him. A shrill of sadness swept down me. Perhaps I was right. Violet *was* embezzling money. Violet *was* gambling on *Celebrity Tango*. David came looking to collect from Violet, and one thing led to another...

Note to self: move to Montana.

Lilly tapped my leg. "You bum is making a noise."

Huh?

Oh, my phone!

"I have to go!" I yelled up to Antonio and slapped my cell to my ear without checking who it was. Surely it had to be Hampton calling to update me on David's arrest and Violet's whereabouts. "Hello?"

"Curious," came Patrick's familiar authoritative tone. "Do I still employ you?"

That felt like a rhetorical question.

I answered anyway. "Yes?"

"Good, because I was trying to figure out why there is no manager at the LA building or the Burbank building and why I have a three-day-old application in my inbox."

The line beeped, and I checked to see who was calling in.

Kevin.

Whatever it was, he could wait.

Ignore Call.

"I'm sorry, Patrick." I swung Lilly up on my hip and hurried home. "It's been busy here. I've done all the background checks on Fox..." *Ahhhh!* Except I hadn't. I never did send in the resident verification.

Crap.

It was like I was subconsciously trying to get myself fired.

"His credit is decent," Patrick said. "Not great. Not horrible either. He has a large balance on an Abercrombie & Fitch credit card. What did you find out?"

Errrrr...ummmm... I wrestled with my conscience.

On one hand: I could pretend I'd done the resident verification and tell Patrick everything checked on my end. Of course, if I did that and Fox turned into a nightmare resident, it would come back to me.

On the other hand: we'd done a complete background check on residents before and they turned out to be psychopaths.

So there was that.

"Cambria?"

...Errrrr...

"Cambria?"

...Errrrr...

"You still there?"

"I didn't do the verification, Patrick! I'm sorry." I followed a resident through the pedestrian gate so I wouldn't have to dig through my bag for my keys. "I dropped the ball, and I will take care of it right away."

The line beeped. It was Kevin, again.

Ignore Call.

Patrick huffed into the phone, and I pictured him rubbing his temples. *"Please* get the verification done now so we can get him moved in."

"I'm on it." I passed Mickey, who was talking to himself, and Silvia, who was talking to Harold, grabbed a soda can out of the bush and tossed it into the trash. "Also, do you know if the apartment is gluten-free? Fox wants to know. He's no longer eating gluten, or eggs, or...a few other things."

...

"Hello?"

I could now picture Patrick staring heavenward. "I have no idea. Tell him not to eat the walls and he should be fine."

I couldn't help but laugh. "I'll email you once I find out about the rental verification."

"Please." His tone was lighter. "Any word on Violet?"

Errrr...ummmm... I wanted to tell Patrick what I'd discovered but ultimately decided to keep it to myself. "They've made an arrest, but as far as I know she's not been found."

"That's a shame. Keep me posted."

I promised to do so and hung up just as Kevin called, again.

"Kevin this isn't a good time." I set Lilly down and dug around in my purse in search of my keys.

"I found your guy." His voice was barely audible over the swooshing of traffic in the background.

"Which guy?"

"Clint Eastwood."

I paused. "Where?"

"You've got to see for yourself."

I rolled my eyes and found my keys. "Can you just tell me?"

"No. You *have* to see this in person."

I looked down at Lilly. Then at my door. Then at the keys in my hand.

I had so much work to do.

CHAPTER NINETEEN

———

—But I went anyway.

The address Kevin gave took us to a 7-11 across the street from County Hospital. He was waiting by his car, wearing his work coverall and sucking down a large Slurpee.

"I'm here." I climbed out of my car, flipped the passenger-side seat down, leaned into the back, and unbuckled Lilly. "Where's the guy?"

A Cheshire cat smile spread across Kevin's face. "You're going to flip out." He reached for his phone, and I smacked his hand.

"You're not recording me flipping out."

"Please," he begged. "This could go viral."

"Is that why you made me come down here?"

He stuck the straw into the corner of his mouth, which answered my question.

Heaven help me. I may smack this man upside the head.

"I doubt whatever you show me will rival the information I've potentially uncovered today." I helped Lilly out of the car and used my hip to close the door.

"We'll see about that," he said, as if challenge accepted. *Great.*

Kevin waved for us to follow. I held Lilly close. The street was busy, and a line of cars waited to turn into the underground parking structure. Nurses and doctors walked to and from the hospital entrance—some staring at their phones, others talking on them. I sidestepped the man asleep on the sidewalk using a newspaper as a blanket.

"Why is he sleeping on the ground?" Lilly pointed.

"Don't do drugs," the man grumbled.

Oh geez.

We stopped at the corner among a sea of people waiting to cross. Downtown Los Angeles smelled like BO, smog, and, now that marijuana is legal, pot. Lots and lots of pot. The light turned green, and everyone walked, except for Kevin. "You ready?" he asked.

"Fine. I'm ready. Is he one of these guys sleeping on the ground? Or that guy over there peeing on the tree? Or…what in the world? Is that dude dressed like Michael Jackson, or is he supposed to be Cher?"

"Monica Lewinsky." Kevin grabbed me by the shoulders and manually turned me around so my back faced the hospital.

"I still don't see him," I said, growing impatient.

Kevin placed his hands on my cheeks and maneuvered my attention upward to the billboard across the street from the hospital.

"Oh…bleep!"

CHAPTER TWENTY

———

—Everyone claims to have an attorney.

"Mother…freakin'…son of a bleeper…" I pumped the gas three times and turned the key. My car started with a *sputter* and a *splat*, and we were off.

"What are you saying, Momma?" Lilly asked from her car seat.

I flipped on the blinker and merged onto the freeway. "Nothing. I'm upset right now."

"Who are you mad at?"

"Humanity?"

"What's hum-an-nan-nin-ity?"

"A species incapable of making good decisions."

"What's *species* mean?"

"I'll explain it to you when you're older." I weaved through traffic, took the next exit, and used side streets to get home. "Flipping…stupid…pee-brained…"

I took a sharp right onto our street and pushed the gate opener stuck to my visor. My right leg bounced, shaking the entire car. Kevin was right. I was flipping out.

I sailed over a speed bump and screeched into my parking spot. In the maintenance garage, Mr. Nguyen looked up from behind the air-conditioning unit he was working on, but I didn't say anything. Not even a hello. I was too upset.

With Lilly on my hip, I marched to the third courtyard and up to the Nguyen's apartment. The door was unlocked, and I let myself in. Mrs. Nguyen sat behind her sewing machine at the kitchen table, hemming a pair of dress pants. I knew without looking there was a pot of pho simmering in the kitchen. Mrs.

Nguyen peered at me over the glasses resting on the tip of her nose. "You look terrible."

Mrs. Nguyen wasn't a beat-around-the-bush kind of woman.

"She's mad at hum-man-nin-ity," Lilly offered.

Mrs. Nguyen looked to me for clarification.

"Can Lilly hang out with you for a few minutes? I need to use adult language."

"Of course. Go. Go." Mrs. Nguyen held out her arms, and Lilly crawled onto her lap. The two conversed in Vietnamese, and Lilly helped press the pedal to make the sewing machine work.

I quickly retreated and soared down the stairs. My jaw tight, hands clenched into fists, and legs still shaking. Never in my life had I ever wanted to punch someone as much as I did in that moment.

Which is saying something.

I'd met a lot of punchable people.

Kevin waited in the middle of the courtyard, hands on thighs, struggling to catch his breath. "Damn, woman, I almost got in a car accident chasing you."

I didn't answer. I ran up the stairs to Larry's apartment and pounded on the door using the inside of my fist until his hoarse voice yelled for me to come in.

Larry's apartment smelled stale. Piles of newspapers and books were stacked on every available surface. A television sat atop a card table, and Larry lay atop a recliner in the middle of the room. Both legs wrapped in hip to ankle braces and a bandage over his nose.

I stood in front of the television, my chest pumped full of adrenaline, and struck a Wonder Woman pose. If only I had a lasso to whip him with. "You hired a lawyer!"

Larry cowered, as if willing himself to blend in with the fabric of his chair. "I'm not allowed to speak to you."

"I went to the hospital, and they told me I wasn't authorized. It's because your lawyer, Brian T. Rains Attorney at Law, aka Clint Eastwood look-a-like, told you not to!"

Kevin stood in the doorway with a smirk on his face. He was enjoying the show.

"I'm...I'm..." Larry struggled to speak. His eyes shifted from Kevin to me and back again.

"For the past three days I've been worried sick about you." Well, not *sick*. But certainly worried. "And your lawyer has been snooping around here. If Kevin hadn't shown me the billboard right outside the hospital, a billboard with Brian T. Rains' giant face plastered across it and the promise to get millions for your personal injury case, then I wouldn't have been able to put two and two together! I can't believe, after living here for as long as you have, that you'd sue Elder Management!"

"I'm not suing Elder Management," said Larry. "They've been great to me."

"Oh." *Oops.*

"I'm suing you," he said.

For a moment, I couldn't even speak.

All I could do was stare.

Until my brain caught up.

Then all I saw was red.

"What!" I exploded. "Why would you sue me? I didn't do anything."

Larry made a steeple with his fingers. "If you hadn't yelled at me, then I wouldn't have slipped on the roof and broken my nose. Which prohibited oxygen to my brain. If I'd had full use of my faculties, then I wouldn't have fallen from the roof."

Correction: never in my life had I ever wanted to punch someone as much as I did in *that* moment.

"What does Daniella have to do with any of this?" I asked. "Why was your lawyer looking for her?"

"As a character witness."

"For whose character?"

"Yours."

Kevin held me back. "You tried to jump from the roof! I stopped you!"

"Like I said," Larry continued, his voice measured, hands still steepled. "I didn't have full use of my faculties because my nasal septum was prohibiting air supply."

He looked like Larry.

He smelled like Larry, but he didn't sound like himself.

It took a great deal of effort to keep my anger at bay. *This can be solved logically,* I thought. Even if Larry didn't have full use of his faculties, an argument could be made he never did.

Brian T. Rains had infested these ridiculous ideas into Larry's head. There was no way he'd come up with it on his own. *Two can play at this game.*

If he was going to be ridiculous, then I was too.

"Fine. Then I'm filing a countersuit against you," I said.

"For what?"

"Your boot hit me on the head, and I now suffer from insomnia." The hope was he'd hear how stupid the accusation sounded and realize how stupid the lawsuit against me was.

No such luck.

"Then I will see you in court."

Ugh! "Larry, I understand you're under a great deal of stress right now," I said. "However, spending your time and energy on a lawsuit you'll end up losing is a waste. Think about how this will play out in court. I tell the judge about the call I received from a resident saying a man was attempting to break into her apartment and how this man had climbed onto the roof. She doesn't know who you are. Then I see someone walking on the roof. Of course I was going to yell at you. I wasn't trying to scare you. I didn't even know it was you. But if you hadn't been on Apartment 15's patio, then none of this would have happened. Heck, if you weren't on the roof, none of this would have happened."

Larry made a *W* with his arms. "What are you talking about? I was never on anyone's patio. I climbed the roof and was going to cross the breezeway and climb down to the walkway on the other side. Why would I go on someone's patio?" he said, as if the concept was absurd.

I stumbled backward. "But...but if you weren't on Julia's patio, then who was?"

"How would I know? I got locked out of my apartment!"

My breath hitched in my throat. *Wha...wha...huh...but...* "I have to go." I huffed out the words.

"Don't leave, Cambria! Wait. Wait." Larry held up a cup and gave it a little shake. "Could you, uh, fill this up for me?"

"I don't know. Will you sue me if I don't fill it up right?"

"It's nothing personal."

"How's it *not* personal?" I barked.

"Please." Larry smiled.

I should have walked away. I should have slammed the door and left.

So I did.

Then I opened the door, grabbed the cup, and filled it up because, I mean, the guy didn't have use of his legs.

I handed Larry the water, snapped a picture of his face with my phone, and ran off. My mind racing.

If Larry wasn't on Julia's patio, then someone else was...there was a man on her patio around the same time Violet went missing...her apartment faces Cedar Creek...someone could have easily climbed on the wall and up onto the patio.

Thru the breezeway and into the second courtyard I went. A group of residents were having a pool party. Large inflatable swans floated in the deep end, and beach balls bounced around. House Rules, page five, paragraph twelve: no oversize inflatable toys permitted in the pool area.

Note to self: deal with this later.

"Wait up!" Kevin came running up behind me. "Where are you going now?"

A beach ball smacked me in the back of the head. "If Larry wasn't on Julia's patio, then someone else was right around when Violet disappeared."

"That's not good."

"No. It's not."

We were at Julia's door. I had no idea if she was home or not, and after knocking multiple times, I realized she wasn't. Kevin and I flew down the stairs and were marching side-by-side to the office when we saw Julia at the mailboxes, sorting through her mail. She had on scrubs with kittens on them, a Taco Bell bag wrapped around her wrist.

"Was this the man on your patio?" Kevin and I said in unison. I had my phone out with the picture of Larry on it.

Julia flatted her back against the mailboxes, a hand over her heart, mail now on the ground. "You scared the crap out of me."

"Sorry," I said. "Is this the man?"

"No."

"Can you look a little harder? Imagine him without the brace on his nose and without the look of shock on his face." I held the phone closer until she went crossed-eyed.

"The dude on my patio looked nothing like this guy. He had a hood pulled over his head, and his face was longer and younger."

I looked at Kevin to see if he was thinking what I was thinking, and since he was already headed to his apartment, I thought we were thinking the same thing.

CHAPTER TWENTY-ONE

———

—Certain situations are beyond profanity.

The three of us sat around Julia's kitchen table. Her brother Kane was home, on the couch, playing a video game. Never acknowledged us. I'd already left two more messages for Hampton. Julia kicked off her shoes and tucked her legs under her butt, with a bean burrito in one hand, a beer in the other, and eyes closed as she tried to remember the facial features of the man she saw that night.

Kevin's pencil danced around the page as he erased and re-sketched. I studied the drawing over his shoulder, watching the lines come together to form the outline of a face, the cheeks, nose, eyes, hairline, chin.

The more the sketch began to form, the more familiarity the picture took on.

There's no way!

I had my phone out, searching the internet. "How do you know this was a man?" I asked Julia.

She shrugged. "Because of the big sweatshirt, I guess. Why? Does it not look like a man to you?"

"It actually looks very similar to this woman." I showed her the picture I found online.

Julia squinted. "Oops. I guess it wasn't a guy. I just assumed it was."

Kevin and I shared a look.

The picture was of Violet.

CHAPTER TWENTY-TWO

———

—As the manager, I can enter the premise without warning in
case of an emergency.
And emergency is subjective.

Kevin, Julia, and I were on her patio, not exactly sure
what we were looking for. The block wall separating the two
properties stopped a foot below the bottom of the patio. If Violet
had stepped on the hood of a car, she'd have been able to climb
up fairly easily—wounded or not.

"She may have been looking for help," I said, thinking
out loud. *Or Violet set this whole thing up to look like she'd been*
kidnapped, when really she was on an island somewhere sipping
water from a coconut, happy she'd escaped prison time, is what I
was thinking inside.

"Crap!" Julia freaked. "And, like, I told her to go away
or I'd kill her!" She sandwiched her cheeks between her hands. "I
mean, I was in the shower and, like, I come out to find this
guy...or *girl*...banging on my window. That's scary. What would
you have done?"

The same thing.

Except I would have called 9-1-1 instead of the manager.

Seemed insensitive to point that out again. "It's not your
fault," I assured her. "There's no way you could have known."

"Cambria, look at this." Kevin pointed to Daniella's patio
directly below us. All the outside furniture was turned on their
sides. Even the charcoal BBQ pit (which are strictly prohibited)
had been knocked over, and ash dusted the concrete.

Note to self: deal with that later.

I rose to my toes and leaned over the railing, nearly giving myself the Heimlich. It was hard to tell from my upside-down position, but there appeared to be glass on the ground as well. A horrid thought trampled into my head.

Daniella never did return my phone call. If Violet had jumped down onto Daniella's patio, and her attacker chased her, or if Violet herself was desperate to get away unnoticed...

"What's wrong?" Julia asked in a panic. "Why are you making that face?" She turned to Kevin. "Why is she making that face?"

"She's thinking," he said.

"What is she thinking!"

I rose upright and waited for the blood to return to my head. "It's fine," I said as convincingly as I could. "I need to speak to Daniella."

And make sure she's still alive.

"But she's, like, out of town on vacation," said Julia, and the relief hit me like a two-ton brick. Except...

"No she's not," I remembered. "She was out of town two weeks ago. I fed her tarantula while she was gone."

"No. She came back from Miami and then left again. She went to Argentina for three weeks. I'm feeding her spider now." She made a face. "Except, crap, I forgot to do it this week. Shoot. I also forgot to let out the cat."

Hold on... "Daniella has a cat?"

Julia slapped her hand over her mouth. "I wasn't supposed to tell you that."

"When did she get a cat?"

"She brought it back from Miami."

"Are you serious—" *Stay focused, Cambria.* "Never mind. Not important."

Not now at least.

I went downstairs. Julia and Kevin followed.

Daniella's blinds were drawn. "And you're positive she is out of town," I confirmed with Julia because I was about to open Daniella's apartment, and if I did so and found her on the other side, she'd berate me, or kill me, or sue me, or all the above.

"Yes, I'm positive," said Julia.

Good enough for me.

I used my master key to open the door and poked my head in, afraid of what I would find. Daniella had a futon instead of a couch and a large dark rug that took up the entire living room floor. Her walls were covered in framed pictures of family and friends and snapshots from tropical vacations. On the entry table sat Gary the Tarantula's cage.

"Are you sure she has a cat?" I asked Julia, who cowered in the doorway.

"Mmmhmmm. Daniella said she brought back a cat from Miami and to let it out when I fed the spider so he could get fresh air. Then she said not to tell you because pets aren't allowed. But then, like, I see pets around here all the time."

"They're service animals," Kevin told her.

"Ohhhhh."

"I don't think she has a cat," I said, surveying the living room. "I typically have a horrible allergic reaction when I'm even in the same... Holy mother of everything that's unholy!" A giant bat-looking creature jumped up on the back of the futon and hissed at me. "What is that thing?"

"It's a hairless cat," Kevin said. "Wow. I've never seen one in person."

"Why is it looking at me like that?" I backed against the wall. "Is it going to attack?"

Kevin extended an arm out to the feline. "Nice kitty."

Nice Kitty bared his teeth and hissed. Kevin stepped outside with Julia. "I'll let you handle this, Cambria."

Gee, thanks.

The cat ran his tongue over his mouth and lay across the back of the futon, folded his paws, and kept his big orange eyes on me.

Please don't let this be how I die.

Cambria Jane Clyne (pronounced Came-bree-a) died, attacked by giant hairless cat.

The patio door was in the kitchen, and I inched slowly, sidestepping on my tiptoes as if I were the Pink Panther. I could almost hear the theme music. T*o do, to do, todo todo todo todo todooooo.*

When I stepped into the kitchen, I saw the broken window. I saw the litter box. I saw the turned over chair. I saw the trail of red. I saw...

"Ahhhhhhhhhhhhh!"

CHAPTER TWENTY-THREE

———

—Murder is an emergency.

A woman in a blue jacket tied the end of the caution tape to a wooden pillar and rolled the rest across the walkway, prohibiting unauthorized personnel from entering. Julia was back in her apartment, drinking. Kevin was sitting against the pool fence, holding Daniella's cat. Violet was in Daniella's kitchen, dead.

I had four thoughts on the subject.

One: Violet had been attacked, left to die, escaped, and run to my community. When she was denied access to Julia's apartment, she tried Daniella's, broke the back patio door, and died in the kitchen before she could get help.

Two: I'd thought I heard someone yelling my name on Monday night. It could have been Violet.

Three: I might join Violet when Daniella finds out about this.

Four: How can I convince both Tom and Chase to move to Montana?

The woman in the blue jacket was back. This time she held up the tape allowing the coroner to pass under. He wheeled a gurney containing Violet. I looked away even though she was covered. The pool party was still going on. The air smelled of chlorine and sunscreen. KIIS 102.7, the local radio station, pumped from a portable radio. Laughter erupted from the woman in a yellow bikini perched on the shoulders of her friend, engaging in a chicken fight—blissfully unaware of what was happening yards behind her.

If only I could live in a state of blissful unawareness.

Also, it would be nice to fit in a bikini.

"Stabbing," Hampton said, and I spun around. His face remained stoic, and his hair remained squirrelly.

"Excuse me?"

"She was stabbed in the back and twice in the side."

Oh.

I fidgeted with the watch on my wrist, making a conscious effort not to vomit, or cry, or both. I'd specifically *not* asked for death specifics because I specifically didn't want to know. I'd already seen too much, and I wanted to sleep again...someday.

"Obviously, she didn't go out any window because the timing doesn't work," I said. "I just don't understand how she managed to get from her apartment to Julia's apartment if she was so badly injured. Why not knock on her own resident's door?"

"There could have been someone chasing her, she saw the light on in Apartment 15, decided to go for it, and that's all she wrote."

"What did she write?" I asked. "Did she leave a note?"

"It's an expression. *That's all she wrote.*"

I just stared at him. This was no time for idioms.

"Never mind," he said. "Truth is, people don't think clearly when they're injured and in life or death situations."

"People don't think clearly regardless." I folded my arms over my stomach.

"There were Twinkie wrappers stuck in her hair," he said. "Quite a few, actually."

"You never responded to my text message!"

"I said there were Twinkie wrappers in Violet's hair, and you didn't even bat an eye."

"I'm an apartment manager. Nothing shocks me anymore. Why didn't you respond to my text?"

"I was in an interview." Hampton cleaned his glasses using the underside of his shirt. "Do you know how we can get a hold of Daniella Lopez?"

I shook my head. "She's out of the country. I've already left her several messages."

"Don't be surprised if she moves after this."

"Really?" I tried not to sound too hopeful. "Have you spoken with the owners of Cedar Creek? Do they know about Star Management? Did *you* know about Star Management before I told you?"

He gave his pants a hike.

I took that as code for *no*.

The LAPD should seriously consider putting me on their payroll.

"We knew she'd filed for a business license in 2011, but we couldn't find any bank accounts linked, and she claimed zero income on her last couple of tax returns. Dick Dashwood, he didn't know about the company," he said. "He did say they attempted to fire her earlier this year. According to him, she was difficult to work with, but her reports were pristine, and she ran a tight ship."

"That's bananas!" Also, brilliant, considering she thought of the scheme on her own.

"My best guess at this point is, she gambled all the money away on horse races and reality shows."

OK, it was just bananas. "So David is her bookie and her killer? How can he collect his money if he kills her? That doesn't make too much sense." Granted, I'd never dealt with a bookie.

"Nothing has been confirmed. But his prints were in the apartment, he has a record, and he's our prime suspect."

"There had to be a second person, right? The window was open, and he ran down the stairwell. Something isn't adding up."

"Agreed. We brought him down for questioning shortly after you left last night, but he hasn't given us anything. We'll break him eventually."

Eventually?

I checked my watch. David had been there for over fifteen hours. If he hadn't confessed by then, I doubt he'd confess at all. Which meant he could not have done this to Violet. Which meant someone else did. Which meant that person could still be around, somewhere.

I thought about Dolores's threat to slice my throat.

I thought about the property owners who wanted Violet gone.

I thought about the non-Floridian daughter who was quick to ransack her mother's apartment after she turned up missing.

I thought about all the residents who'd received rental increases shortly after moving in.

There were quite a few people who had motive to kill.

Or…it was David, and he was immune to Hampton's interrogation skills. They needed someone more versed in psychological tactics. A detective with the ability to manipulate. The ability to intimidate. The ability to properly wear hairpieces.

Speaking of intimidate and manipulate and inability to wear apparel. Silvia Kravitz approached. Her silk robe open and flapping at her sides. Harold on her shoulder, wings out and flapping at his sides. "Apartment Manager! These people are being so loud in the pool, and they're not allowed to have those large… What is this about?" She pointed to the crime scene tape.

Hampton made himself scarce.

"We had an…um…incident," I said.

Silvia brought her hand to her chest. "First there's a creepy man looking in our patios, and now this! How many people are going to die before you get fired? It's like I'm living an episode of one of those trashy crime shows you watch."

"How do you know what I watch?"

"Because your television faces the window. Everyone knows what you watch."

Note to self: keep blinds drawn, always.

"The man you saw was Larry's lawyer," I assured her. "It has nothing to do with what happened here."

Silvia shook her finger at me. "No. No. No. Everyone knows Brian T. Rains. His commercials air during *Wheel of Fortune*. The man I saw was no lawyer. He was trouble. Probably a friend of yours."

"No he wasn't. I don't have friends." That came out wrong. Anyway. "What did this guy look like?"

"He was about this tall." She held her hand just above her head. "He had dark hair and was wearing a shirt with *Vegas* printed across the front and *Went on Vacation, Came Back on Probation* written on the bottom."

Definitely not something a lawyer would wear.

Not a smart one anyway.

I rubbed my temples. "Did he have sleeve tattoos and look like a young Bob Saget?" I asked.

"How am I supposed to know that?" Silvia huffed. "All I know is, he was peeking into windows like a complete pervert."

"How many times did you see this happen?"

"Tuesday, late afternoon." She held up one finger. "Wednesday, midmorning." Two fingers. "Last night." Three fingers. All three fingers an inch from my nose.

"Why didn't you call me last night?"

"Because obviously our safety is not your concern."

Good grief!

I called Hampton over. "Silvia, Detective Hampton. Hampton, meet Silvia and Harold. She has information for you."

I walked away, and a beach ball smacked me in the back of the head, again. I kicked it, meaning to send it back over the fence into the pool, but it landed squarely in Kevin's face.

"What was that for?" He flung the ball in the air and spiked it back. I dodged out of the way, and it went whizzing past me and rolled down the breezeway, stopping at Chase's feet.

Chase!

"I leave for three days, and CSI is..." he started to say, when I buried my face into his chest and inhaled his familiar sexy man scent. He wrapped both arms around me and held tight. The situation suddenly felt less horrid.

"I found Violet dead in Apartment 15," I mumbled into his chest.

Chase didn't speak. Instead, he squeezed me harder. I peeked over his shoulder at Hampton. Silvia waved her hands around, retelling the tale of the pervert in Vegas clothing. He nodded along. Her perv sounded a lot like David. He was a bookie. Which meant he had most likely spent time in Vegas. He didn't strike me as a perv, but I doubt he was looking for anything pervy—more so looking for Violet.

My best guess: she had escaped after he stabbed her. Not sure where the Twinkie wrappers came into play. Perhaps she was stress eating when David approached her, and she fell onto her discarded wrappers, and they were entangled in her hair before she ran off. He had no idea where exactly she went but knew she couldn't have gone far. Which led him to my place. He had to find the body before anyone else did.

Again, my best guess.

Also, my head hurt.

"I see Hampton has met Silvia," Chase said with a chuckle. "Poor man."

Poor man indeed. Except, "Is he *blushing*?"

Chase squinted. "He is. But Silvia looks like she's about to cry."

"No, that's what her face looks like when she smiles."

"Her cheeks are red, too."

"Oh my gosh. She just touched his shoulder. I've never seen her touch anyone before...holy crap." I gasped. "He's holding Harold? Silvia doesn't let anyone touch her bird, and Harold bites...ewww. Did Hampton just..."

"Yes, yes he did." Chase lowered his head.

"He kissed the bird," I whispered in shock. "On the beak, and Harold didn't bite him."

"He's an animal lover."

"This is getting weird."

"Agreed."

"But I can't look away."

"Me either."

Hampton and Silvia were flirting with each other five feet from a murder scene.

The two went together like ketchup on a banana.

Cheese Whiz on Frosted Flakes.

Pineapple on pizza.

Grandma Ruthie used to say, "Attraction is a funny business. Don't try to make sense of it. Just go with it."

Good news: if they fell in love and got married, Silvia would move in with Hampton and I would no longer be her apartment manager!

Or...

Bad news: he'd move in with her.

Hampton returned Harold and walked toward us. Silvia moved on to Kevin. No flirting this time. She waved her arms around, complaining about his hairless companion.

Chase and I just stared at Hampton as he approached.

"What?" he asked.

"How'd you get Silvia to like you?" I asked in awe.

"She's a nice, perceptive woman," he said.

Perceptive: yes.

Nice: no.

"Her description lines up with David," he said and extended a hand to Chase. "Did you just get back?"

"Landed less than an hour ago. Anything I can do to help?"

"I've got it all under control," he said with more confidence than I'd ever heard before. With reason, I supposed. He had a body, and he had a suspect.

The optimist in me was relieved.

The pessimist in me knew this was far from over. Nothing in my life ever appeared as it seemed. There was always something or someone lurking around the corner ready to rear his or her ugly head. It was just a matter of whose head it would be.

Also, if my mind were a pie chart:

70% worst-case scenarios

20% optimist

10% ice cream

So who knew how this would turn out.

CHAPTER TWENTY-FOUR

———

—The definition of a polyp

We were back in my apartment before five. Chase and I sat on the couch, while Lilly played with the plush airplane he'd brought back for her. "Momma, watch." She held the toy high above her head and made the *whooshing* noises of a plane gliding through the air. It was cute until she crashed the plane into the wall and sent it spiraling to the floor, where it exploded with fiery sound effects.

I really need to get this kid socialized before she buys a ferret.

"Thanks for my toy." Lilly gave Chase a hug. "It's more fun than rice!"

Chase looked to me for clarification.

"I'll fill you in later," I said.

"Glad you like it, kiddo." He kissed the top of her head, and she continued to crash her plane.

I snuggled closer to Chase and rested my head on his shoulder. Life felt more manageable with him around. The stress of all the murders and lies and unauthorized pets melted away. If only for a moment. He was warm and kind and easy.

Not easy, *easy.*

Not like man-whore easy.

My relationship with Chase was not a nauseating roller coaster. It was more like a gondola ride down a smooth canal.

And I could use more gondolas in my life.

There was no question about where he stood. No question if he did or did not have feelings for me. No question about any of it.

Well, except one.

"Can you come to New York with me if Amy makes the finals?" I asked.

"When is it?"

"A week from Monday."

He rubbed the back of his neck. "I can make that work."

"Good." I settled back on his chest, when another question trotted into my head. "How many kids do you want?"

"Why do you ask?" His eyes went to my stomach, and I sucked in my gut.

"I don't want kids," Kevin announced. "They're messy."

Oh yeah, Kevin was there. He was sitting at the kitchen table eating a yogurt, with his feet propped up on a chair.

"My uterus has polyps," Mrs. Nguyen said.

Oh yeah, Mrs. Nguyen was there too. She was perched on the other side of the couch with a fan positioned in front of her.

"What's a polyp?" Lilly asked, still flying her plane across the room.

"It's like a…a…" *I'm stumped.*

"It's a growth?" Chase said.

Lilly nodded, thought this over, and then asked, "What's a growth?"

"It's something that has grown off the skin or an organ, like a tag," Chase said.

Lilly nodded, thought this over, and then asked, "What's a uterus?"

Chase squeezed my knee. "I'll let you handle this one."

My head was too murky and my heart too heavy to talk female anatomy. "How about we eat sugar?" I suggested instead, and the subject was instantly dropped.

"Yay!" Lilly flew her plane to the kitchen, and I took a head count for ice cream cones. All hands went up except for Chase. His pie chart didn't include ice cream.

I grabbed the box of waffle cones, package of brownie bits, and tub of double fudge. I began assembling by shoving bits of brownie into the cone, to keep the ice cream from dripping out the bottom. A trick I'd learned from my Grandma Ruthie.

She was basically a genius.

I ran my ice cream scooper under the hot water and glanced out the window. Hampton entered the first courtyard from the parking area, and we locked eyes. He gave a slight nod of his head, and I knew he'd been over to Cedar Creek to talk to Stormy and Antonio. My insides shriveled, thinking of how they took the news.

"Kevin, can you take over?" I passed him the scooper, and he sprung into action, making perfectly round mounds of ice cream.

I reached for my keys, but Chase snatched them off the counter before I could grab them.

"Where do you think you're going?" he asked.

"I'm going next door to check on the staff. They just found out their manager was found dead. That's a lot to take in."

"Give them time to process. You can stop by before we go."

Go? "Where are we going?"

"Out to dinner. You need to get off this property, for awhile at least."

True.

CHAPTER TWENTY-FIVE

———

—It's hard to keep track of all the vendors.

I gave Stormy and Antonio an hour to process. Chase came with me, and we walked the ten-yard journey hand-in-hand. Six o'clock, and cars paraded down the street, ignoring the twenty-five mph limit. I waved to each passing vehicle. All were residents arriving home from a day's work. I could picture Silvia standing in the carports, arms crossed, foot tapping, face frozen, eager to tell everyone about the missing property manager found dead in Daniella's apartment. As a retired actress, she had a gift for storytelling.

And exaggeration.

"Watch your step." I pointed to the curb in front of Cedar Creek so Chase wouldn't trip like I had many times.

He laughed, like I'd made a joke. "The large *Watch Your Step* sign and the bright red curb gave it away."

Yeah, OK, whatever.

Must be nice to be coordinated.

Chase stopped to admire the koi pond. "I remember checking this place out when I worked undercover."

"Did you meet Violet?"

"She gave me a tour." He dipped the tip of his finger into the pond, and a bright orange fish came to the surface.

"Did she offer you a month-to-month or a year lease?" I asked.

"She offered month-to-month only on certain apartments."

I shook my head. And at the four-month mark she'd give the option to pay more or sign a lease. Who wouldn't sign the lease? Too bad she didn't use her genius for something worthwhile. Like...gee...I don't know...her job. "It's hard to believe she was able to get away with it for so long."

"Considering what happened, I don't think she got away with anything."

The image of Violet in Daniella's kitchen popped into my head, and I quickly shook it away before the nausea set in.

I'll never eat Starbursts again.

I entered the code Dolores had given me into the intercom. "Be prepared," I warned Chase and opened the door. The lobby was less icebox and more Antarctic. The news of Violet's death had traveled fast. Vases of beautifully arranged flowers lined the lobby and office with baskets of fruit mixed in.

So I guess *now* would be the appropriate time to bring a fruit bouquet.

Everyone had hurried to give gifts of condolences, and my hands were empty. All I had was Chase. Knowing Stormy, she would appreciate a man more than flowers anyhow.

The office was empty. The digital time floated across Stormy's computer screen, and a file box sat atop her desk, open and empty.

"Why is it so cold in here?" Chase cupped his hands and breathed into them.

"It happens when you reach a certain age." I peeked around the corner down the hallway. The storage closet door was open. "Hello! Stormy?"

She poked her head out and smoothed down her hair. "Oh heavens me, Cambria. I didn't hear the intercom." She had another file box by the handles and was carrying it down the hallway.

"We used Dolores's code. Sorry." I pointed to Chase. "This is my boyfriend."

Confusion plagued her face, and she slid the box on her desk. "This is your boyfriend?"

Chase extended a hand. "Chase Cruller."

Stormy slipped her hand into his, keeping her eyes on me. "Nice to meet you, *Chase*," she drew out his name.

"How are you doing?" I gave her a hug. She smelled of coffee and paper.

"I feel terrible. Just awful. Sick even. I can't believe this has happened." She slumped down into her chair. "The detective asked me about leases and a management company? I don't know anything of it. I don't know what I'm more upset about. That she was killed or that she'd been stealing money." She grabbed a large iced coffee from under her desk, wrapped her lips around the straw, and took a sip. Leaving behind red lip prints. "I guess I'm more upset about the murder," she decided.

"How is Antonio doing?" I asked.

"He took the news hard. I think we were all holding on to hope she'd return."

"Is there anything we can do for you?" Chase asked.

She refused to make eye contact with him, which didn't seem like her. She'd about imploded when she found Kevin on my...*gawk!*

No wonder Stormy appeared confused. The last time she saw me, I was with a shirtless Kevin and he'd declared we were having...

I choked on my own spit and hunched over in a coughing fit. Struggling to catch my breath. Chase patted my back, and Stormy scooted off to the Wow Fridge and returned with a bottle of Cedar Creek water. She twisted off the lid and held it up to my mouth. Bless her heart, she figured me as a two-timing hussy and didn't say a word to my real boyfriend.

The water helped ease my lungs. I pounded my chest with my fist, swallowed a few times, took a few breaths, and gulped a bit more water. Then I spoke. "There was a misunderstanding the other night," I started. "Kevin, the man you met, we weren't...you know."

Now both Chase and Stormy stared at me.

Oh geez.

"I mean...it was all...just a..." What was I supposed to say? Kevin lied so she'd leave? There was no winning here. I polished off the water bottle instead.

"I'm not sure what you're talking about." Stormy winked.

Oh hell.

"What are you doing?" I pointed to the empty boxes, to change the subject.

She glanced down at her desk, as if just remembering, and re-slumped into her chair. "I'm packing."

"Did you get fired?"

"Not yet. But with everything that happened with Violet, I doubt they want me to stay on. I doubt I want to stay on. I thought property management would be fun and, honestly, *easy*. I had no idea it was so...so..."

"Stranger than fiction," I finished for her.

She gaped at me. "Yes! I don't know if I can sit across from Violet's desk without thinking about what happened either." She shuddered.

I grabbed one of the empty boxes and placed it on the floor. "I wouldn't start packing right now if I were you. You've kept this place going during this horrible time, and you should stay on, at least until the owners replace Violet. That way you can get a reference. You could get a job at a smaller community to start. One like mine."

Stormy picked up her coffee. "Like yours? Are you quitting?"

"No, it was an example. Mine's only forty units. Then I also manage another place in Burbank that is only..." Crap! Fox! I never finished his application!

Stupid. Stupid. Stupid.

However, in my defense, the dead body I'd found distracted me.

Patrick was reasonable. He shouldn't be upset.

However, in his defense, this was the second dead body I'd found since I began working there.

Perhaps I should be the one packing file boxes?

"Anyway." Stormy dropped her chin into her palm. "I better get back to work."

"Of course." I gave Stormy a hug. "Call and let me know how you're doing."

"I will," Stormy promised.

Chase placed a hand on the small of my back and led me toward the door. *Oh! Wait!* I spun around. "Do you mind if I take a picture of the Wow Fridge to show my boss?"

"Be my guest," she said.

Chase heaved a sigh.

"What's your deal?" I asked under my breath. It wasn't like him to be so pushy.

"Sorry. I'm hungry."

"This will only take a minute." I opened the fridge.

"Wow," Chase said from over my shoulder.

"Exactly." I pulled the water bottles forward to make a perfect line and turned my phone vertical to snap a picture. "When this case is all done…" I turned around to be sure Stormy couldn't hear. She was secluded in the office, filling her boxes, out of earshot. "I was thinking about setting Stormy and Hampton up." I turned my phone horizontal and adjusted the lighting. "Don't you think they'd make a cute couple?"

Chase shrugged. "She looks too young to be having hot flashes."

"What do you know about hot flashes?"

"When you're a detective, you learn things you don't want to know," he said. "Are you almost done?"

"Almost." I swiped through the pictures to make sure I captured the *wow*. Because I'd have to *wow* Patrick in order to get a *Wow* Fridge added to the budget.

"What's Stormy's story?" Chase asked.

"Same ole', same ole'. Moved to Los Angeles to become an actress, settled for a mediocre paying, soul-crushing job instead."

"How'd she have no idea Violet was embezzling money if she's the assistant manager?"

"Violet wouldn't allow her to do any of the managing." I placed my hand in his and intertwined our fingers. "We can go now."

Chase opened the whimsical door for us. We stepped into the summer air and strolled down the walkway.

"Now that we're alone, can we go back to the kid thing?" Chase asked.

Oh, right. "What are your thoughts? Not that I want to have a baby right now. It's just that we've never talked about it."

Chase came to a stop at the red curb and massaged the back of his neck. I braced for the bad news soon to follow. "I need to tell you about my special assignment."

"Crap. You got someone pregnant!"

"What? No."

"You found out about a secret love child in Texas?"

"What? No."

"You—"

He pressed his finger to my lips. "I applied to the FBI."

"What's that have to do with kids?"

"If we're talking kids and marriage, we need to be completely honest with each other."

My heart lurched. *Marriage.*

Who said anything about marriage?

Well…I guess I did, when I mentioned more children.

I supposed matrimony would be the logical first step.

A step I skipped over the first time.

Chase wasn't a skipping (or falling) over steps kind of guy.

"I can tell you're angry," Chase said.

Angry? I wasn't angry. I should be angry he didn't tell me about applying to the FBI. But life is short. People die. *A lot.* Specifically around me.

No time to be upset over career advancements.

"It's incredibly competitive, and I didn't know if I would get in," Chase explained. "Or if I wanted to get in. That's why I was in Texas. It was phase three of my interview process."

"Phase three? Why didn't you tell me about phases one and two? How many phases are there?" And also, "What's a phase?"

"I applied before you and I began dating. I didn't hear anything until about three months ago. I got a call to meet with an agent in LA. Then I took the test, and this past weekend I flew out to do a meet-and-greet and final interview. I should have told you, but I didn't want to worry you."

I shook my head, trying to understand. "When do you find out if you got it?"

"I did. Now I wait to see when I start training. It could be three months. It could be ten months. I've heard for some it takes over a year."

I didn't know much about phases or what exactly it meant for him to be in the FBI, but it sounded exciting. I was about to give him a hug and tell him congratulations—

"Nothing has to change between us," he quickly added before I could get the words out. "I plan to keep working until I get training orders. I had no idea how badly I wanted the job until I was at the final interview yesterday." Two creases appeared across his forehead. Two I'd never seen before. And I realized, Chase was worried that I'd be upset he kept this from me.

And my stomach lurched again.

I need to tell him about Tom.

But first.

I swung my arms around his neck and kissed him. My heart pattered in my chest, and my cheeks went hot, and my legs went goo.

I'll kiss him once. Then I'll let go. Then I'll tell him about the kiss I shared with Tom in the bathroom.

He shouldn't be too upset. After all, it was Tom who kissed me.

Mostly.

Also, Chase and I hadn't been a serious couple at the time.

Mostly.

Denial can be a powerful thing.

Almost as powerful as the connection Chase and I shared.

Oh my.

"I take it you're not upset with me," he said against my lips.

"I guess not. FBI agent sounds kind of hot.

"Good." He sighed, and the creases disappeared. "I've been wanting to tell you since I got home."

"Is that why you were so anxious to leave?"

"Yes, and it's like ten degrees in there."

I let out a laugh. "Are you still taking me to dinner?"

Chase snaked his arm around my waist. "Anywhere you want to go."

Anywhere?

Hmmmm...

If I had my choice of any restaurant in Los Angeles, I'd pick Bottega Louie. Avocado and Chorizo toast on fresh, homemade bread, along with a variety of melt-in-your-mouth macaroons.

But tonight wasn't about me. Chase was now, or was about to be, in the FBI, and I had to tell him I kissed my baby daddy. So, "Hollywood Pizza."

Chase gave me a look. "You want to go to Hollywood Pizza?"

"Why wouldn't I?"

"The last time we ate there, you said the crust tasted like tree bark and you were one hundred percent positive the sauce was Ragu."

That sounded like something I'd say. But still, "I feel like tree bark Ragu tonight. Plus, there's something I want to talk to you about too."

"Does it have to do with kids again?"

"Not necessarily." Though, when he said kids, it reminded me. "Shoot. They have the cutest kids' corner at Cedar Creek, with coloring books and toys. I want to re-create something similar, and I forgot to take a picture of it to send to Patrick along with the Wow Fridge."

"Can't you Google *kids' corner* and send the link to Patrick?"

I paused.

Sure.

But…

"If he sees what our next-door competitors have, it will have a bigger impact. I'll be right back. Get in the car, and I'll meet you in there." I kissed him on the cheek and ran back to Cedar Creek, skipped over the step, and my knee buckled.

Son of a… I hobbled around, muttering to myself, until I was able to move my leg again.

Note to self: see a doctor, woman!

I didn't want to bother Stormy, so I used the code Dolores had given me.

Access Denied

Weird.

I tried a few more times without success. Lucky for me, a resident exited, and I was able to slip right in. The office was empty. I snapped a picture of the kids' corner from a few different angles, then swiped through my pictures to see if I'd done it justice. The pics were dark, and I looked up. The track lighting over the table had two light bulbs out.

I sent Antonio a text and snapped one more picture.

He replied back almost instantly: *Who is this?*

Me: *Cambria. I'm in the lobby.*

Antonio: *I think you have the wrong number.*

Me: *No, this is Cambria Clyne, from next door. Two light bulbs over the kids' corner are out.*

Antonio: *Cambria Clyne the apartment manager?*

Geez. The man had short-term memory.

Me: *Yes.*

Antonio: *You manage the place off Sepulveda Blvd?*

OK, this was getting ridiculous.

Me: *Yes*

Antonio: *I don't do light bulbs. How's the new window?*

I checked the front window.

Me: *The window looks good.*

Antonio: *If you ever need another let me know. I gave Mr. Nguyen a quote to put new windows in every apartment if you're interested.*

I was confused, so I called him.

"Hey there, Cambria." It didn't sound like Antonio at all.

"Who is this?" I asked.

"It's Antonio from MM Glass Repair."

I looked down at my phone. Mr. Nguyen had sent the contact as Antonio MM, and I assumed MM meant maintenance man. He'd obviously sent me the wrong Antonio.

"Did you get a message from me a few days ago?" I asked.

"You're right. I did. I didn't recognize the number, and the message didn't make any sense so I figured it was a mistake. Do you need a new window for an apartment with a leak?"

"No...but if I called you then, how did Antonio know to meet me at Violet's apartment?"

"I'm not sure what you're talking about."

"Sorry. I'm thinking out loud."

"We have a special on double pane right now..."

Antonio MM continued his sales pitch, and I mentally put him on mute. If Antonio at Cedar Creek didn't get my message about the leak in Violet's bathroom and Dolores was unable to get a hold of him, then why was he on his way to Violet's apartment to fix it?

CHAPTER TWENTY-SIX

———

—*Things are never quite what they seem.*

Monday night I'd been so consumed with the leak, and my knee, and Larry who had just fallen off the roof, and David who had just run me over in the stairwell that I didn't pay attention to much else. But when I closed my eyes and removed all other distractions from the equation, I was able to pick up on few things.

1) Dolores *did* say when we talked on the phone that her son was with her, helping her collect the water dripping from the ceiling.

2) It's unlikely David would flood his own mother's apartment. Even more unlikely Dolores would involve me if her son had just killed the manager. When we spoke, she sounded genuinely desperate to stop the leak. However, it was possible she didn't know her son had killed Violet until after we hung up.

3) David could have called his mother after he kicked in Violet's door, suspecting he was standing in a crime scene. That was when they decided they didn't want to risk being involved at all, since David already had a record.

4) I had run into Antonio. In such a hurry, I never did ask if he received my voicemail. I assumed he had, since he was there. And Dolores said she didn't have his number. How else would he have known?

Crap.

Stormy!

She still wasn't in the office. The boxes were half full, and her ice coffee sat atop the desk—a condensation ring formed around the bottom. I ran down the hallway and checked the storage closet and the bathrooms. She wasn't there, but the door to Antonio's office was cracked open.

I crept along with my back against the wall and peeked into the sliver of an opening. Antonio had a tight grip around Stormy's arms and had her pressed against a filing cabinet. She let out a yelp.

I started to call Chase, then hung up. Figuring I should take my own advice.

In case of emergency...

"9-1-1 what's your emergency?"

Antonio's office fell silent. He had his hand pressed over Stormy's mouth, and his ear pointed in my direction.

I hid behind the blue cabinet in the hall and pulled my knees to my chest. The door opened, and I imagined Antonio poking his head out. Afraid he'd hear the operator, I hung up the phone and curled into a tighter ball.

"Hello?" Antonio called out. "Hello?"

I bit my lip. Afraid I'd answer.

Per Hampton: people don't think clearly when they're in a life or death situation.

This felt very life or death-ish.

The door closed. I remained in a ball and composed a text message to 9-1-1, giving the address, description of the suspect (Antonio), and the hostage (Stormy). I had no idea if 9-1-1 received text messages or not, but in a day and age when people used their phone more as a flashlight than to make actual phone calls, you'd think texting would be an option.

Placing my palms on the fancy rug, I went to my knees and crawled toward Antonio's office. I couldn't leave Stormy. I couldn't barge in either and risk getting killed. I was a mother. I had a kid and a boyfriend who wanted to marry me...someday. Maybe. Hopefully.

A loud crash came from the room. It sounded like a large piece of furniture had been thrown to the floor. I pictured Stormy fighting for her life, and my brain abandoned all sense of reasoning. I rose to my feet and...crap.

CHAPTER TWENTY-SEVEN

———

—Gravity is not my friend.

I hit the floor with a thud and got a rug burn along the palms of my hands on the way down. It wasn't even my knees' fault. I'd tripped.

On air.

Up again on two feet, I charged toward the office and turned the knob as I rammed my shoulder into the door, thinking it would be locked, thinking I possessed the superhuman ability to bust open a locked door.

PS: I don't.

I do, however, have the ability to bust open an *un*locked door and send it crashing against the wall. Having used all my strength, the momentum propelled me forward, and I slid across Antonio's desk like it was home plate.

Smooth.

I scrambled to my feet and...*holy hell.*

No. No. No

I covered my eyes and screamed. "Doesn't anyone have sex in the privacy of their own home anymore!"

"Oh my heavens. Don't you know how to knock?" I heard the distinct sound of a zipper being pulled up.

I turned around and faced the opposite direction. An old poster of Cindy Crawford holding a Pepsi can plastered one wall. I concentrated on Cindy.

"What the hell are you doing here?" Antonio asked.

"Errrr..." Blinded by naked Stormy and Antonio, I'd completely forgotten why I barged in.

Ummm...cell phone...wrong number...how did Antonio know about Violet's apartment...right

Since Stormy was obviously not in harm's way.

Since Antonio was obviously busy.

Since I was obviously not needed in that moment, I backpedaled toward the door, fidgeting with my fingers.

"Wait, Cambria." Stormy stood in front of Cindy. Her shirt on backward, pants unbuttoned, lipstick smeared across her mouth. "What's wrong?"

"Errrr...I heard a crash."

"Oh, you sweet thing." She smoothed her hair back into place. "That must have been the toolbox." She giggled. "We got a little carried away, and it tipped over. See, I was feeling so sad about Violet. Antonio was feeling so sad about Violet. I came to comfort him and—"

"Don't need specifics."

"Let's just say there actually are men my age who *can* keep up." She winked.

Gross.

There was a very real possibility the worst-case scenario part of my brain took over and I had this all wrong. So I might as well ask. "Antonio, how'd you know about the flood in Violet's apartment if you didn't get my voicemail?"

He pulled up his pants. His chest still bare of clothing and the cross around his neck still tangled in hair. "A resident told me there was water coming down from Apartment 105's ceiling, and I figured it was coming from Violet's."

"Oh." Made sense. Made perfect sense.

Well, that was embarrassing.

My phone buzzed. It was Chase. I answered. "Sorry. I'm on my way."

"You OK?"

"Yep. I'll be there in a sec." I hung up and rocked from heels to toes. Stormy and Antonio still staring at me.

This is awkward.

"Sorry. You two can...continue...I'm going to...just..." I cocked my thumb to the door. As I turned, my eyes swept the office. On the floor was a mess of files that had slid off the desk when I made my grand entrance.

On top, the file for Apartment 105, Dolores Rocklynn, lay open. Her assigned entry code, the one I had used earlier, had been whited out and a newly assigned entry code had been written in red.

They'd changed Dolores's code so I couldn't enter.

Or so David couldn't enter, I reminded myself. When I'd mentioned I knew Dolores's code, Stormy could have been worried about who else had it, given the situation with David, and changed it while it was fresh in her mind.

It was what I would have done.

Except...

The manila folders beneath Apartment 105's were for apartments 306, 402, 610, 509, 508, 404, 903, 314, 407, 612, and 101. The tabs were written in the familiar chicken scratch.

Stormy's chicken scratch.

Violet had swirly writing.

Stormy said they didn't keep paper files.

Still, there could be a reasonable explanation for why Stormy had the files. Hampton asked for them, and she gathered all the information she could find and placed them in new folders. She and Antonio could have been working on the project together, when one thing led to another and...oops. Their clothes fell off.

Denial can be a powerful thing.

I backed away. "I'll leave you two to...continue." I grabbed hold of the door to close it and took note of the circular hole where the knob had crashed through the drywall when I'd burst in. "I'll...um...pay for that."

Antonio's shirt was stuck beneath the door, prohibiting its closure. I yanked it free and handed it to him, not making eye contact. He slipped the shirt on over his head without a word.

Neither he nor Stormy said a word.

They didn't need to.

The words on Antonio's shirt said it all. *Vegas! Went on Vacation, Came Back on Probation.*

CHAPTER TWENTY-EIGHT

———

—Some like it rough.

There was no denying it. Antonio was taller than Silvia, he had dark hair, and more incriminating, he had the black shirt matching Silvia's description. A shirt with holes on the bottom and white paint smudges on the shoulder. Obviously, his work shirt. He was the one looking in patios and peeping through windows. He was the one looking for Violet. *Crap.* If only I'd been around to see him, then I could have put this together sooner.

Except...

Silvia said the man was there Tuesday evening. Wednesday midmorning. And Wednesday night. I realized, every time Antonio was snooping around, I was preoccupied.

I was preoccupied by Stormy! She'd called about the virus. She called when her icons disappeared. She showed up at my doorstep with flowers. After I received Silvia's call on the emergency line and tried to leave, Stormy was desperate for me to stay. I thought it was because she didn't know what she was doing. In reality she didn't want me catching Antonio snooping around my apartments. He was looking for Violet.

I've been played.

I'd been played so badly I didn't know whether to laugh or cry. I thought Stormy was an untrained assistant manager in over her head. I thought Stormy desperately needed my help. I thought Stormy was my friend. No wonder the office was at sub-zero temperatures—she was a sweaty-mess liar.

Just like Violet!

Never in my life had I ever wanted to beat the crap out of someone as I did in that moment.

Luckily, the reasonable side of me took over before I got myself in trouble.

And the reasonable side of me goes by the name of Chase.

"Cambria, there you are..." Chase must have felt the tension in the room, because he stopped midsentence and did a quick scan of the office, from the folders on the floor, to Stormy in her backward shirt, to Antonio, to Cindy on the wall proudly holding a Pepsi.

I didn't know what to say or what to do. From the look on Stormy's and Antonio's faces, they knew that I knew, and they knew that I knew that they knew. From the look on Chase's face, he was putting the pieces together.

So we all sort of stood there.

"We're going to be late for dinner," Chase said causally.

"You're right," I said, equally casual. "We have reservations."

We turned to leave.

Antonio leapt in front of us and kicked the door shut. In one quick swoop, he had me in a bear hug with a sharp knife at my throat.

Where was he hiding this knife?

I'd seen the man naked ten minutes ago.

Kevin was right. You can stash a weapon anywhere!

Chase didn't react. Like me being held hostage, with a knife to my throat, was neither surprising nor alarming.

I, on the other hand, was reactive. I wouldn't consider myself proficient in the human anatomy. But I was pretty sure nothing good happened when a knife sliced through your carotid artery. The more I struggled to break loose, the tighter Antonio held. "He killed Violet," I rasped. If I was going to die, I might as well get the truth out.

Chase cocked his head. "Let her go."

"Antonio!" Stormy cried. "Antonio, don't hurt her!" She dramatically sunk to the floor and hysterically screamed into her hands, a performance worthy of a daytime soap.

Antonio ran the tip of his knife under my chin, and I felt a drip of blood trickle down my neck. I closed my eyes.

"Let her go," Chase demanded again.

I could feel the perspiration seeping through Antonio's shirt and the beads forming on his arm. He didn't answer Chase, but his breath quickened. I wondered if this was how it ended for Violet.

My mind raced through every single crime show, hostage situation, and YouTube video I'd seen, but I had no idea how to get out of a knife to the throat. What I did have was an FBI agent standing in front of me. Granted, he had not been trained yet. Also, I had no idea if he was armed.

"My name is Detective Chase Cruller with the LAPD. I'm wired, and there is a SWAT team waiting for you outside that door," he said. "You drop the girl, and we go peacefully."

He was bluffing. Unless I'd missed something.

Stormy screamed. "Oh my heavens! Heavens no! No!" She rose to her knees and clasped her hands. "Help us, please! Help!"

Chase produced a gun out of, what felt like, thin air. Because apparently everyone has had weapons hidden in their nooks and crannies but me.

Chase had a gun aimed at Antonio.

Antonio had a knife on my throat.

If Stormy produced a weapon, we were both screwed.

"Drop your gun, or I'll kill her," Antonio said. "I'll slice her neck, and she'll be gone in thirty seconds."

On TV, when the criminal had the girlfriend hostage, the cop would drop their weapon and back away slowly with their hands up, ready to negotiate.

Chase doesn't watch enough crime shows.

Instead of dropping his weapon, Chase said, "You kill her. I kill you."

I liked the television version of this scenario better.

"I'll do it," Antonio said. "I'll kill her right now!"

"How is killing Cambria going to get you what you want?" Chase asked. "She's the only thing keeping you alive right now."

Antonio's grip around my neck loosened, but the knife remained pressed against my neck.

Stormy remained on her knees, silently pleading, or praying, or both.

Chase remained in wide stance, gun drawn, and finger on trigger.

I remained lucid, which is saying a lot because it took every ounce of willpower I had to not freak out. In a situation such as this, I assumed I'd be the hero. I assumed I'd be able to disarm the perp. But kicking and thrashing around didn't seem like the right approach for a man holding a sharp object to my major artery.

Unfortunately, kicking and thrashing was my only idea.

A commotion outside caught my attention. It sounded like an army was fast approaching, or a charge of angry residents.

Antonio turned his head in the direction of the noise, and his grip loosened enough for me to slip out. No sooner did I move, than a shot was fired and Antonio dropped to the floor.

"No!" Stormy screamed. "Oh heavens no!" She crawled toward Antonio until Chase told her to be still.

The door kicked open, and, sure enough, a SWAT team arrived. Chase had been right.

Or, 9-1-1 had received my text.

Either way, I made a shield with my hand, not wanting to see Antonio on the ground. I had no idea if he was dead or alive. On TV he would be alive but injured, but this was clearly not one of my "trashy" crime shows.

Chase spoke to the team of men and women entering the tiny room. I caught every few words, my heart still pounding in my ears. "Drawn down...Hit the X..."

Stormy was still on the floor, with her hands over her face, crying. I couldn't understand why no one had cuffed her. Until Chase said, "...both hostages uninjured..." and I realized Chase thought Stormy was a hostage, not an accessory.

In my text I'd said as much.

They didn't know what I did.

My theory was confirmed when Chase lowered to one knee and placed a comforting hand on Stormy's back. She continued to cry, shoulders shaking, body sweating, shirt still on backward.

Chase stood, and Stormy peeked up at him, tears streaming down her cheeks, disdain on her face. She reached under the desk and produced a small silver pistol.

"Watch out!" I grabbed Chase by the shoulders and shoved him out of the way. The gun went off, and that was about all she wrote.

CHAPTER TWENTY-NINE

———

—Almost

When Amy and I were kids, we'd close the door to my room and flip the light switch on and off so fast it looked like a strobe light. We'd strike silly poses and dance around. Our movements appeared to be in slow motion, and we thought it was hilarious. Light on: one pose. Light off: Light on: new pose. Light off.

That was what being shot felt like.

Minus the hilarious.

Light on: Stormy against the wall with her hands cuffed. Light off.

Light on: Chase's face, lines creased across his forehead. Light off.

Light on: a stranger saying my name.

Light off.

Light on: four bright fluorescent lights, the sound of a siren, and the slight jerking of movement.

Light off.

Light on: Brian T. Rains' giant face looking at me through the window.

Light off.

Light on: rectangular ceiling tiles.

Light off.

Light on: Chase at my side, smoothing an ice cube over my lips like he was applying gloss. I waited for the light to turn off again, but it remained on. I ran my hands along the stiff, sterile fabric of hospital sheets.

"What happened?" I asked, feeling groggy. It was a fight to stay awake.

"You were shot."

"Shot!" My hands went to my chest. I checked my arms. Felt my head. I could move my feet and my toes. "Where was I shot?"

"In your butt."

My butt?

I wiggled a bit.

Yep, that hurts.

Good thing I had padding there. Guess ice cream can do a body good.

"Did I lose a lot of blood?" I asked. "Why is there an IV in my arm? Why is my head so foggy? How did I get in a hospital gown? Did they do surgery? Did I lose a lot of blood? Why is there an IV in my arm?"

"You have a concussion." Chase dropped the ice cube into a paper cup. "You pushed me out of the way and fell against a filing cabinet and hit your head."

Got shot in the butt. Ended up with a concussion. Sounded about right.

"Where is Stormy?" I asked.

"In custody. She confessed to killing Violet."

I couldn't have heard him right. "Stormy killed Violet? I thought Antonio did."

"No. Stormy and Violet were in on the con. They embezzled close to a million dollars over the last three years. Prior to Stormy working there, Violet made about forty grand extra a year renting out one apartment. Enough to support her gambling habit. Then Stormy came on and beefed up the business. Violet paid her a third of every rental."

A third?

If only my head weren't so foggy, then I'd be able to do that math.

That was a lie.

Even when I was drug free, I still wasn't great at math. But I thought about the Post-it notes on the bottom of Violet's monitor. The tally marks. About a third of the rent would make sense. She'd kept track of what she owed Stormy.

"With the property owners doing an audit, they knew there was a good chance they'd get caught. Stormy wanted Violet to take the blame," Chase continued. "She went to Violet's apartment Monday night and found Violet on the toilet with the bathtub running. Violet was upset because she'd lost the last of the money to a bad bet. The two argued, and Stormy stabbed Violet, several times. Thought she'd killed her and called Antonio for help. The two were *involved*."

"Yeah, I saw." I saw *everything*.

"Together they put Violet in a plastic tub—"

"Did they use a dolly to take Violet down to the parking lot?" I interrupted, suddenly remembering the tire marks near the baseboard and the dolly underneath the stairwell.

"How'd you know that?"

I tapped my temple, and then forgot what we were talking about.

Um...

Right. Violet. Dead. Dolly.

"They put the plastic bin in the back of Stormy's car. Ran back upstairs to clean up the mess, but they couldn't get the bathtub to shut off. The plan was to pack all Violet's stuff into a suitcase and make it look like Violet took off. But when the bathroom began to flood, Antonio ran to get his tools."

"And *that's* when David showed up. Stormy hid while he tried to turn off the water. Then I came into the picture," I said with a shake of my head. "Antonio did announce our arrival before we entered, giving Stormy enough time to escape."

"Exactly. Stormy climbed out the window, went down the fire escape, and drove home. When she got home, she realized Violet was no longer in her car. Violet wasn't dead, obviously, and had managed to escape. Jumped on the patio of Apartment 15, and you know the rest."

Yes, I did. And to think, Stormy would have gotten away with it if it weren't for a faulty bathtub lever. There was still one question, though. "I get why no one would bat an eye when the maintenance man hauled around a big plastic bin. But, how did Stormy climb down the fire escape and no one noticed?"

Chase shrugged.

Geez. There was no way Stormy would get away with that on my property. If a resident so much as sneezed too loud, Silvia called to complain.

Guess there are benefits to having a community busybody.

"What was with the Twinkie wrappers?" I asked.

"Violet was eating them before Stormy showed up. She's a stress eater."

I could relate.

Must be a manager thing.

Not sure there were enough calories available to help me stress eat my way out of this debacle though.

"I can't believe she confessed to everything," I said.

"It was all Hampton," Chase said, like a proud papa bragging about his son. "Ten minutes in a room with him, and you'll confess to anything."

I shook my head. Not sure I heard him right.

But Grandma Ruthie did used to say, "Can't judge a book by its cover."

Maybe behind the high pants and squirrelly hair was a master manipulator, intimidator, and...*ugh. My head hurts.*

Where was I?

Right.

"So Stormy is in custody, and Antonio is..."

"Dead."

Oh.

Antonio died, and he wasn't even the killer. I felt guilty for about ten seconds. Then I remembered he tried to kill me. Then I didn't feel so guilty anymore. Then the guilt returned. I never wanted anyone to die.

Speaking of death. I felt like I might. "Is the gunshot wound deep?"

"They were able to easily remove the bullet. You have two stitches."

Two? I get shot, and all I got is two measly stitches?

"Why do you look disappointed?" Chase asked. "Were you hoping for more?"

"No, I guess not." Two stitches, an ambulance ride, and a stay in the hospital was going to cost me enough. "Where is Lilly?"

"With Kevin and Mrs. Nguyen. She's fine."

Chase stood and placed the cup on a tray. For the first time, I noticed the curtains drawn around my bed and paid notice to the noise around me. "Am I in the emergency room?"

He nodded. "I'll tell the nurse you're up and making sense again so we can get you discharge papers," he said.

Discharged? "Getting shot is outpatient?"

"Around here it is."

"Have you ever been shot?" I asked.

"No, I haven't."

"At least today gave you good practice for the FBI." I tried to make light of the situation, because there was nothing light about Chase, from the frown on his face to his rigid stance. This wasn't the easygoing gondola Chase I was used to.

"We'll see," he said. "The watch commander hasn't relieved me. I'm on paid leave until the incident is reviewed. Not sure how this will affect everything."

"What are you talking about?"

"I killed a man today, Cambria. It has to be investigated. Standard procedure."

Oh. "I'm sorry."

"Don't be. You took a bullet for me today." Chase studied the ceiling. "I just don't understand why you put yourself in these situations. You obviously knew Stormy and Antonio were involved in Violet's murder. You had the sense to text dispatch but not the sense to keep yourself out of it."

"I thought Antonio was hurting Stormy."

"I understand that. Which makes this ten times more infuriating because I can't even be mad at you for wanting to save your friend."

"A friend who turned out to be a psychopathic murderer."

Chase ran his hand down his face. "Will you please, from now on, take your own safety into consideration? Please?"

"Yes." I made a cross over my heart.

"Good." Chase kissed my forehead. "I'll get the nurse." He drew back the curtain, revealing a busy ER. Nurses and doctors rushed around, sorrowful-looking individuals lay on gurneys, and police paced the narrow halls.

Nausea crashed over me, and I draped my arm over my eyes.

I hate hospitals.

The headache, the stomachache, the buttache, none of it rivaled the pain I felt knowing this incident could have been avoided had I left well enough alone, though. Had I stayed hidden behind the cabinet and not run into Antonio's office, he might still be alive. Chase wouldn't be on paid leave. Stormy and Antonio would have both had their day in court, and I'd be at home.

Note to self: stop solving murders.

I needed a new hobby, like crafting, or blogging, or needlepoint, or antiquing.

With my arm still draped over my eyes, I heard the curtain close. Chase grabbed my hand and held it close to his chest. Except it didn't feel like Chase. I lifted my arm. "Tom, what are you doing here?"

"Mr. Nguyen called me."

I moaned. Chase was already upset with me—the last thing the situation needed was my baby daddy. "Tom, I'm—"

He shushed me. "Don't speak. Save your energy, sweetheart."

Sweetheart?

Tom kissed the backside of my hand, and I peeked up at the bag attached to the IV pole next to my bed, wondering what was in it.

"You scared the hell out of me, Cam." Tom knelt at the side of my bed, still holding tight to my hand. "We'll get you the best care. Don't worry."

"I'm not worried," I said. "I was shot in the butt and have a minor concussion. Chase went to get the nurse so I can be discharged."

Tom blinked a few times. "That's not so bad," he almost sang.

Easy for him to say.

"Mr. Nguyen said you'd been shot and were rushed to the hospital," said Tom. "I didn't pay attention to anything else and got into my car and rushed here."

"I appreciate the gesture, but I'm going to be OK." I tried to pull my hand free, but Tom wouldn't let go.

"No you won't. We've been through way too much over this past year, and I'm sick of it."

"Don't worry," I said. "I'm seriously considering retirement. Except I'm not sure what else I could do."

"I do." Tom cupped my face gently in his hand. "I'll get a job at a bigger firm and take on paying clients. You can stay home with Lilly, or go back to school, or get a job where people aren't constantly trying to kill you."

OK. This had to be the pain meds. But just in case it wasn't, "Can you repeat that?"

"Cam, I want to have a life together. I want our family together."

Chase is a liar!

He lied to me. Two stitches and a minor concussion? There was no way. I must have lost half-a-body worth of blood, and hit my head hard enough to cause a brain bleed, and be on enough drugs to where I was hallucinating, because it sounded an awful lot like Tom was...

"I love you, Cambria," he said, and my heart skyrocketed into my throat.

The room spun, and I wasn't quite sure what to say or what to do or if this was even real.

"You don't have to say anything now." He stood and ran a hand through his mane. "Just think about it. We could get out of LA and go someplace where you can buy a house for less than a million."

"Like Montana," I said.

"I was thinking more like Inland Empire or Fresno. I don't want to take the bar again. But we can talk about it." He unleashed his flirty side smirk, and I was reminded of the night we met.

The curtain flung open, and Chase stood beside a woman wearing blue scrubs. "Tom," he said. "I didn't know you were here." He forced a smile.

The nurse removed the needle from my arm and replaced it with a piece of gauze. "Are you ready to go, dear?"

My eyes cut from Tom to Chase and back again.

"No."

CHAPTER THIRTY

———

—Leaving the property in the hands of someone else while you're on vacation is much like dropping your child off at day care for the first time.
You just cross your fingers everyone will behave and your kid won't bite anyone.

One week later.

"You're not going to a funeral." Mrs. Nguyen picked up the black dress I'd flung into my suitcase and returned it to my closet. She reappeared with my blue Anthropologie dress I reserved for interviews and first dates only. "You look good in blue." She folded it carefully and placed it in my suitcase. "I still can't believe Amy made it to the finals," she said, shaking her head.

"What does New York look like?" Lilly asked.

I folded my jeans into thirds and placed them beside my blue dress. "It's a big city with *really* tall buildings and the Statue of Liberty."

"Do they have donuts there?" Lilly asked. "And ice cream?" She cared more about the food than the landmarks.

Obviously we shared the same DNA.

The office phone rang, and I patted down the bed, searching for the cordless phone, and found it under a blanket. "This is Cambria," I answered.

"We're at the building in Burbank, and we'd like to see a two-bedroom apartment. Do you have any available?"

"We do." I went to the bathroom and collected my toiletry items. "Apartment 21C is a spacious two-bedroom apartment with two bathrooms and ample closet space. The door is unlocked, and applications are on the counter. Please let me know if you have any questions."

We hung up. Every morning, I'd unlock the vacant units, tidy them up, then return later in the evening to lock the door. I'd found it easier to leave the vacant units open and applications available than to sit in a hot closet the local teens used as a brothel and wait for prospective renters to show up.

Rather genius if you asked me.

Also, the residents there hated me.

With a passion.

Yes, they'd rectified all infractions, but they'd bashed me on Yelp, Apartment Ratings, and Rent or Run dot com, and now gave me evil stares when I was there. The iron fist approach did not work out so well.

Not so well at all.

I dumped my toothpaste, toothbrush, and mouthwash into a Ziploc and grabbed my makeup bag.

"What's this for?" Lilly held up the inflatable butt donut and stuck it on her head like a crown.

"For me to sit on in the plane," I said.

"'Cause of your hurt bum?"

"Yep. My hurt bum." I wasn't looking forward to the six-hour flight. Now I understood the appeal of a high-tech toilet seat.

I finished packing and rolled my suitcase down the hall. "You're sure you'll be OK manning the office while I'm gone?" I said to Mrs. Nguyen. I'd decided to use my vacation time, leave a day early, and spend a full week in New York.

"I can handle it. No problem."

"I made you an instruction manual for while I'm gone." I grabbed the binder on the kitchen counter and flipped to the table of contents. "I made a tab for each day. What to do in case of an emergency, and under *Emergency* I have subtabs: *Fire*, *Murder*, *Flood*, and *Lockout*."

"What's PIMA mean?"

"Aw yes." I flipped to page twenty-two. "PIMA stands for pain in my…" I glanced down at Lilly. "*Bum.* Here you'll see Silvia, of course. Though she's been less grouchy since she began seeing Hampton."

"I never would have put those two together," Mrs. Nguyen said.

"You and me both, but he's been here every night this week." He'd show up around sunset with flowers in hand and wig on head, then leave around sunrise the next morning.

"He's too young for her," Mrs. Nguyen said.

"If he's happy and she's quiet, I don't care what the age gap is between the two." I flipped the page. "And there's Daniella."

"Does she know about the dead lady in her apartment?"

"Not yet. She's still out of the country and not answering her phone. I left her a detailed voicemail. Julia said she's supposed to return home any day now. So...um...good luck with that."

"And Larry." She pointed to his name.

"Aw, Larry. He can now hobble around his apartment, so he shouldn't call you for help."

"Is he still suing?"

"Yes, but not me." He'd called the day after I was released from the hospital and asked for me to fill up his water for him. I refused. He apologized and said he'd decided to sue the manufacturers of the boots he was wearing instead. If the boot hadn't fallen off, then he'd have been able to walk the roof more adequately.

I gave up trying to understand.

"The last on the list is Fox. He's the new resident in Burbank. He's not so much a pain as he is obnoxious. He gives his keys out to his girlfriends-of-the-day then asks to get his locks changed when he dumps them. I told him to use a locksmith, but it doesn't stop him from asking anyway."

The bell chimed from the lobby, announcing a visitor. I started to go, and Mrs. Nguyen stopped me. "Vacation officially starts now. Let me handle it."

I gave her a hug. "Thank you."

She padded off to the office, and I checked my phone to see how far away my Lyft driver was.

"Will you bring me back a present?" Lilly asked.

I mocked offense. "Do you think I'd travel *all* the way to New York and not bring you back a present? Why do you think I'm going?"

"Can it please not be rice?"

"I promise." I picked her up and kissed her cheeks. Man, I hated leaving her, but I needed this vacation. It had been a hellish year. I'd been responsible for putting several individuals behind bars, and I only hoped they were all in separate prisons and weren't able to communicate or start an I Hate Cambria Club and plot their revenge.

Yikes

Mrs. Nguyen returned. "There's a man and woman here looking for you, Cambria. They say it's important."

I thought about the club. "What do they look like?"

"Old and rich."

To my knowledge, I'd not put anyone old and rich in jail. Not yet anyhow.

Waiting in the lobby were a man with white hair and a pink polo vest over a plaid shirt and a woman with a bob of gray hair, pearls, and a cardigan tied around her shoulders. I'd never seen them before in my life.

"I'm Cambria Clyne. Can I help you?" I said.

The woman spoke first. "My name is Patricia Dashwood, and this is my husband, Dick. We own Cedar Creek Luxury Living next door."

So these were the Dashwoods. Oddly, they looked exactly as I pictured them.

Old and rich.

"I'm so sorry about everything." I gestured to the couch, and they each took a seat.

Mrs. Dashwood crossed her ankles and rested her hands on her lap. "We heard about your involvement in catching Stormy and Antonio," she said. "We're embarrassed to say we had no idea what our employees had been up to. Violet was so difficult to work with that we found it easier to stay away and let her manage than to get too involved."

"You should consider using a management company. They have more checks and balances," I said, thinking of how much Patrick would like to get his hands on that property.

Mr. Dashwood opened his mouth, about to speak, when Mrs. Dashwood tapped him on the knee, and he snapped his mouth shut. "We don't need a management company," she said. "We just need to be more involved. Right, dear?" She looked at her husband.

"Right," he replied.

She shifted her focus to me. "Which is why we're here." *Ugh. Please tell me they're not suing me.*

"How many units is this place?" she asked.

"Forty."

Her face fell. "How long have you been managing?"

"Not long, honestly," I answered, unsure why they were asking, still scared she was about to serve me papers. "This is my first place, and I manage one in Burbank, too."

Mrs. Dashwood perked up. "You manage two properties?" She glanced at her husband. "We'd like you to interview for the property manager position next door."

I nearly fainted.

"We pay very well," she said. "If you get the job, you'll get a discounted apartment should you choose to live on-site. We'll be hiring a new leasing agent and maintenance supervisor as well, obviously. Which, we would allow our new property manager to interview first. It's important everyone work as a team."

I had no idea what to say. My plan was to quit, not get promoted. "When are you interviewing?" I asked.

"It's going to take awhile to figure out this *mess*. We plan to start the interview process next month. If you're interested, please send me your resume."

She handed me a business card with her email address on the bottom.

Dr. Patricia Dashwood, PhD
Licensed psychiatrist

I walked them out and slipped the card into my back pocket. Should I decide not to interview for the position, it didn't seem like a bad idea to have the number for a psychiatrist handy. Not in this business.

"Who was that?" Mrs. Nguyen asked as soon as I stepped back into my apartment.

"The Dashwoods. They want me to interview for Violet's job."

"You'd actually consider going next door after what happened to their other manager?" Mrs. Nguyen asked.

I looked over at Lilly, who was hanging upside down off the side of the couch watching television. "I don't know if I'm cut out for property management. I don't know what to do about anything, to be honest. I hope this vacation will bring me clarity." My phone buzzed. My Lyft had arrived.

I gave Mrs. Nguyen a hug and Lilly a kiss good-bye. I wheeled my suitcase through the office, out the front lobby door, and down the brick walkway. A gray sedan waited at the curb, and I compared the driver behind the wheel to the picture on my Lyft app to be sure it was the same person.

All appeared well.

I placed my luggage in the trunk.

"Cambria!"

I knew that voice.

Crap.

I slammed the trunk closed. Standing on the sidewalk was Daniella, wheeling her own suitcase behind her. "Cambria!" She held her phone in the air, waving it around like she just didn't care. "I get your messages. Where is my cat?"

"We've been over this. You're not allowed to have pets. Did you not get my other messages?"

"Yes, some man is looking for me, and a lady died in my apartment," she said, as if it was of little consequence.

So close…so close to getting away without having to tell her.

Ten more minutes and she'd have to take this up with Mrs. Nguyen. She was nicer to Mrs. Nguyen. Everyone was.

I took a deep breath and gave the spiel Hampton had me rehearse. I told her CSI did a full sweep of her apartment, since it was a crime scene. I told her the apartment had been released, and Mr. Nguyen fixed her window, and we hired a professional biohazard cleaning company to take care of the mess. I apologized for the inconvenience and offered to give her a glowing recommendation should she choose to move.

"I'm not moving. I want to keep my cat."

Crap.

I opened the car door. "You can't keep the cat. This is a no-pet property. We placed the cat at a very nice animal kennel. You can get the specifics from Mrs. Nguyen. I'm on vacation." I slipped into the back seat and closed the door.

Daniella tapped on the window. "You can't take a vacation. We need to talk about my cat."

"Please go," I told the driver, and he pulled away from the curb and drove away.

I leaned my head back, closed my eyes, and mentally switched my brain into vacation mode.

CHAPTER THIRTY-ONE

———

—I am resilient.

If there is such a place as hell, I imagined it would look like LAX on a Saturday. Cars bumper to bumper, cutting each other off, and driving like drunken snails around the departure circle. Horns. Busses. Cop cars. Charter busses. Limos. Planes overhead. Hordes of stressed and tired travelers. Ticket lines zigzagged a mile long. Groups of smokers huddled in the permitted smoking area, blowing nicotine into the air for all to breathe.

I stood under the Delta sign and waited for my travel companion, anxious to get going. This vacation couldn't have come at a better time. My life was a mess. It wasn't just my job either. Even though I had no idea if I was going to continue managing, switch careers, or go back to college. The Dashwoods' offer certainly threw me for a loop. More money. More responsibilities. Nicer apartment. A gym. It would be a huge promotion. I didn't gamble or embezzle, so I wasn't concerned about ending up like Violet. The fact no one noticed Stormy climbing down the fire escape, told me there was no Silvia Kravitz there.

A major plus.

Then there was still the matter of Chase and Tom. Chase had been cleared of any wrongdoing and was off probation. Still no word on when FBI training started. Tom had not wavered in his feelings or gone looking for other female companions to fill his time (like he normally would). It was so like him to waltz into my life and declare his love as soon as I'd given up on the idea.

It was impossible to know what to do.

I'd spent the last 168 hours agonizing over the decision until my mind was made up.

An Uber car pulled up to the curb with the man who'd be accompanying me to New York. He stepped from the vehicle and threw a backpack over his shoulder.

"You didn't have time to change your clothes?" I asked.

Kevin looked down at his coveralls. "No. I rushed straight from work." He pulled a duffel bag from the back seat. "I had to quit."

"You quit your job?"

"My boss wouldn't let me have a week off on such short notice."

"You need a job more than you need a trip to New York. What about rent?"

Kevin slammed the car door shut. "Are you my apartment manager, or are you my friend on this trip?"

"Friend, but when I asked you to come, you said taking time off work wouldn't be a problem."

"And it's not. We can stay as long as you want," he said with a smile. "I don't know why you're upset. If you'd given me more than a day's notice, then I wouldn't have had to quit."

I pulled the handle of my suitcase up. "Amy didn't let me know about the extra ticket until yesterday." We walked into the airport and found a kiosk to print our boarding passes.

"Is Amy going to introduce me to her partner?" Kevin asked.

I scanned my confirmation code. "I told you he's married."

"So what. She can still introduce me." Kevin put his phone under the scanner, and his boarding pass printed.

We took the escalator to the second floor. By some crazy miracle, the security line was short and we walked right up. I took off my shoes, put them in a bin, and placed it on the conveyor belt to be X-rayed.

Kevin tossed his shoes and backpack into a bin. "We're not sharing a room, right?"

"The show is paying for two hotel rooms for three nights." I put my suitcase, purse, and butt donut into a bin. "Then we're sharing a room for the rest of the week. But I got us two double beds." I stepped through the metal detector and was given permission to grab my belongings.

Kevin was plucked from the line for a "random" search and escorted behind a curtain. I sat on a hard plastic chair and waited while they went through his luggage and swiped a wand over his body.

"This seat taken?"

I peered up. "Guess not." I moved my purse. "Kevin is getting extra love from TSA right now."

"Lucky man." Chase sat and stretched his legs out in front of him. "It could be awhile. You want to grab lunch? They have a Hollywood Pizza here."

"Or we could eat this boarding pass and save ten bucks."

"You're funny." He helped me up and grabbed my suitcase. "There's an ice cream place around the corner."

"Sounds perfect." I slipped my hand into his and enjoyed the warmth of his touch. Chase was lucky to get three days off work to spend in New York with me...and Kevin. Amy was able to get an extra ticket last minute.

Was Chase the man for me?

He might be.

Was Tom?

I had no idea.

Grandma Ruthie used to say, "Trust your gut."

And my gut was scared Tom would change his mind a month down the line. My gut wasn't sure it was worth the risk of losing Chase forever. My gut was confused. So I continued my relationship with Chase like the conversation between Tom and me had never happened. Would that decision eventually blow up in my face?

Only time would tell.

Until then... "I'll have one scoop of double fudge and one scoop of mint chip."

ABOUT THE AUTHOR

Erin Huss is a blogger and best selling author. She can change a diaper in fifteen seconds flat, is a master overanalyzer, has a gift for making any social situation awkward and yet, somehow, she still has friends. Erin shares hilarious property management horror stories at *The Apartment Manager's Blog* and her own daily horror stories at erinhuss.com. She currently resides in Southern California with her husband and five children, where she complains daily about the cost of living but will never do anything about it.

To learn more about Erin Huss, visit her online at:
https://erinhuss.com

Enjoyed this book? Check out these other humorous mystery reads available in print now from Gemma Halliday Publishing:

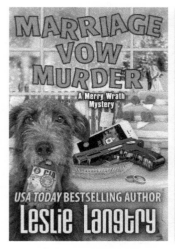

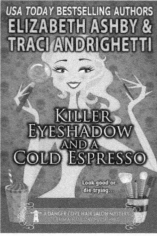

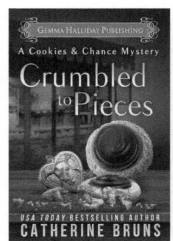

www.GemmaHallidayPublishing.com

CPSIA information can be obtained
at www.ICGtesting.com
Printed in the USA
LVHW041711130219
607433LV00002B/202

9 781793 882561